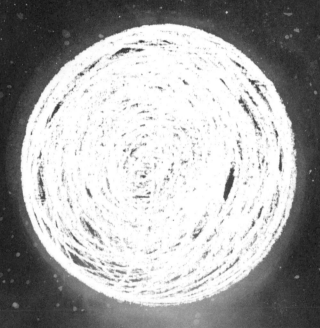

ABOUT THE AUTHOR

Sarah Crossan has lived in Dublin, London and New York, and now lives in Hertfordshire. She graduated with a degree in Philosophy and Literature before training as an English and Drama teacher at Cambridge University. Sarah Crossan won the 2016 Carnegie Medal, the YA Book Prize, the CBI Irish Children's Book Award and many other prizes for her novel, *One*.

sarahcrossan.com   @SarahCrossan

PRAISE FOR SARAH CROSSAN

One

Winner of the CILIP Carnegie Medal
Winner of the YA Book Prize
Winner of the CBI Book of the Year Award
Winner of the CLiPPA Poetry Award
Winner of the Children's Choice Award

'*One* broke my heart and mended it'
Cecilia Ahern

'Tremendously moving and there will be tears'
Toby Clements, *Telegraph*

'One of the most powerful as well as the most
unusual novels of the year'
Independent on Sunday

'An inspiring and beautiful book'
Irish Examiner

'It will shake up preconceptions and move readers to tears'
Sunday Times, Children's Book of the Week

'Truly remarkable'
Irish Times

'The best book I've read in years. It's a spectacular testament to love.
It blows your head back'
Katherine Rundell

'Page after page resonates with exact observation and
lyrical awareness. So, how come it has space and light in it
too? How does it manage to be a page-turner and also leave
room for the reader to imagine beyond the story? Perhaps
because it's written by a very good writer indeed.
I urge you to read this book. Seduction guaranteed'
Jenny Downham

'A heartbreaking and beautiful exploration of how
closely one's own identity is entwined with the lives
of those we love'
Non Pratt

'In short: brilliant. It's truly amazing'
Brian Conaghan

'Quite simply an achingly sad and beautiful story about
what makes any of us human'
Telegraph

'Both lyrical and accessible, this book will draw you in and
break your heart. Sarah Crossan's writing is incredible,
and *One* is simply stunning'
Robin Stevens

'So perfect it hurt to read. A beautiful, lyrical love story
for our time. A definite future classic'
Nikki Sheehan

'This is a strikingly brave, sensitive and unusual book that
packs such a powerful emotional punch, I defy anyone
not to weep at the end'
Daily Mail

MOONRISE

SARAH
CROSSAN

BLOOMSBURY
LONDON OXFORD NEW YORK NEW DELHI SYDNEY

Bloomsbury Publishing, London, Oxford, New York, New Delhi and Sydney

First published in Great Britain in September 2017 by Bloomsbury Publishing Plc
50 Bedford Square, London WC1B 3DP

www.bloomsbury.com

BLOOMSBURY is a registered trademark of Bloomsbury Publishing Plc

A CIP catalogue record for this book is available from the British Library

Hardback ISBN 978 1 4088 6780 8
Export ISBN 978 1 4088 7843 9

Typeset by RefineCatch Limited, Bungay, Suffolk
Printed and bound in Great Britain by CPI Group (UK) Ltd, Croydon CR0 4YY

1 3 5 7 9 10 8 6 4 2

For Jimmy Fox

THE FIRST CALL

The green phone
on the wall in the hall
hardly ever rang.
Anyone who wanted to speak to Mom called her cell.
Same with Angela.

I listened to the jangle for a few seconds
before picking it up.
'Hello?'

'Joe?' It was Ed.
He hadn't been in touch for weeks.
I'd started to worry,
wondered if he was ever coming home.
'Is Angela there?' he asked.
He was breathing fast
as though someone were chasing him.
In the background
        hard voices,
            a door slamming.

'Angela's at soccer practice,' I said.

'And Mom?'

'No idea.
Hey, Ed,
I found a baseball glove at the park.
Will you be back soon to play?'

Ed sighed heavily. 'I dunno, Joe.'

'Oh.' I picked at some peeling paint on the wall.

Another sigh from my big brother.
'I got arrested, Joe.
They think I done something real bad.'

I pressed the receiver tight
                against my ear.
'What do they think you done?'

'They think I hurt someone.
But I didn't. You hear?'

'Yeah.'

'I mean it. You hear me?
Cos people are gonna be telling you
all kinds of lies.
I need you to know the truth.'

The front door opened and Mom stormed in
carrying a bag of groceries
for my sister to conjure into dinner.

'The police got Ed!' I shouted.

      I held out the phone.
           She snatched it from me,
              dropping the bag.

A tangerine rolled across the rug.
I picked it up,
the skin cold and rough.

'Ed? What's going on? …
But how can they make that sort of mistake? …
Don't shout at me, I'm just …
No, I know, but …
I don't have the money for …
Ed, stay calm …
I'll call Karen. I said I'll call Karen …
Stop shouting at me …
Ed, for Christ's sake …
I'm just not able to … Ed? Ed?'

She held the phone away
            from her ear and scowled
            like it had bitten her.
'The cops are charging him with murder,' she said.

I was seven.
I didn't know what that meant.
Did he owe someone money?
We hadn't any cash to pay the electricity bill.
My sneakers were so small
they made the tips of my toes white.
'Can I call him back?' I asked.
The tangerine was still in my hand.
I wanted to throw it in Mom's face and hurt her.

'No,' she said.
'And don't expect to speak to him for a long time.'

I didn't believe her.
I thought Ed would call.
I thought he'd come home.

But he never did.

SLUM LANDLORD

Aunt Karen told me not to come here.
She said Ed didn't deserve an entourage
after the pain he'd caused our family.

Even after ten long years
she blames him for everything.
   She points to Ed and says,
    'See what he did to us.'

And maybe she's right.
Everything turned to shit
when Ed got put away;
nothing worked any more.

So maybe this *is* a stupid idea.

I'm already pining for home, Staten Island,
anything that isn't Wakeling, Texas,
in the broiling heat.

It's not as if I *want* to be here,
checking out some slummy apartment.
But I can't afford to keep staying at
the Wakeling Motorstop Motel,
not for the whole time I'm in Texas anyway.

'Six hundred for the month,' the landlord croaks,
coughing up something wet and
spitting it into a Kleenex.

Judging by the dishes in the sink,
the apartment hasn't been lived in for months and
he'd be lucky to get a dime for this hole –
roaches in the closets,
rodents in the kitchen.

'I need it until mid-August.
I'll give you four hundred,' I say.

He snorts. 'Five hundred. Cash.'
And I can tell by the way he's
        backing out of the apartment
        that it's as low as he'll go.
Well, I guess he's the one with the keys;
he can afford to play hardball.
'If I find out you been selling weed,
I'll send my men round.
You don't wanna meet my men.'

But his men don't bother me.
I got bigger worries
        than getting bashed in with a baseball bat
by his hired goons.

I got Ed to worry about.
        Ed.

So here I am.
        Stuck.

And it's going to be the worst time of my life.
The worst time of everyone's lives.

        For those who get to live.

TEXTS

In the parking lot of my motel
a gang of bikers are slugging booze from paper bags,
hellfire rock music filling up the lot.

As I pass them, my cell phone pings in my
back pocket.
I don't bother checking the message.
I know it's Angela pestering me:
>   Where r u?
>   Did u go 2 the prison?
>   U seen Ed??
>   Hows Ed???
>   Karens still srsly pissed off.
>   Eds new lawyer emailed. He seems smart.
>   Where R U???

I have to call my sister.
And I will.
>   Later.
Right now, I'm starving.

And I have to get away from this music.

BOB'S DINER

The diner is all beat up outside,
paint crumbling, half the neon sign unlit,
and inside it's the same:
broken floor tiles,
posters pale and torn.
A middle-aged waitress in a
pink bowling shirt smiles.
Her name – *Sue* – is embroidered into
her front pocket,
the black thread unravelling itself,
> snaking down the shirt like a
> little vine.

'You OK, hun?' she asks,
raising her hand to her mouth,
dragging on a cigarette right there
behind the counter
like it's totally normal –
> a waitress smoking in a restaurant.
And it might be.   Around here.

I pull out my remaining cash and wave it at her.
'What would four bucks buy me?' I say.

9

'I guess you could get a bacon roll
and a coffee.
Would that work, hun?'

'Great,' I say, inhaling the
        tail of her cigarette smoke.

She shouts my order through a swing door,
turns back to slosh coffee into a stained mug
        and pushes it across the counter.

It's thick and bitter, nothing like you get in
New York,
but I don't complain.
        I tear open a Splenda,
                tip it in to disguise the taste.
'Any jobs going?' I ask.

        'Wait there, hun.'
Sue vanishes
                through the
swing doors.

I grab a muffin in plastic wrap from a basket
on the counter, stuff it into my bag before
        a man appears,

a thick moustache hiding his mouth,
a belly that bulges over his waistband.

He reaches across the counter, shakes my hand.
'I'm Bob. I believe you're lookin' for work.'
His accent is drawn out and totally Texan.

'Joe Moon,' I say.

He nods.
'I need a delivery guy.
Someone with a car, cos the junker
out back won't run.
Or someone real fast on a bike.
The fast person would also need a bike.'

'I fix cars,' I say quickly.
'If I get it to go, could I have the job?'

Sue has reappeared, a fresh cigarette limp
        between her twiggy fingers.
She spits bits of tobacco on to the floor.
'Just so's you know, hun, my boyfriend Lenny's
good with motors. Even he couldn't get that
crap heap to turn over.'

She uses a sour rag
to wipe coffee stains from the countertop.

'I could try,' I say,
not wanting to sound too desperate.

'OK. You can *try*,' Bob says.
He reaches into the basket and
hands me a blueberry muffin.
'Dessert's on me, son,' he says.

NO SHORE

All last week
Reed tried to cheer me up.
Sitting in his car drinking warm beer,
he tried to make me believe Ed would get off,
that I'd be back in Arlington before
the track and field holiday programme
began.
'I'll win bronze for steeple chase,
you'll get a gold for five thousand metres.
Then we'll go to the shore
and show off our medals.
We can stay at my cousin's beach house
as long as we want.
We'll get tans,
        smoke dope,
                hit on hot girls.
So many hot girls at the shore.'

'Sounds good,' I said,
knowing it was never gonna happen,
knowing I'd miss out on my entire
summer,
including the New York City
track and field programme.

It was the one thing that had kept me going
in school –
>   knowing that at the end of the year,
>   no matter how low my grades were,
>   I'd have the programme to prove
>   I wasn't some layabout loser.

But instead of running,
I was coming to Texas
to count down the days until
my brother's execution;
trying to make me feel better about that
was pointless.

THE SECOND CALL

I liked cheese sandwiches with a truckload of ketchup
and had a plate of them in my lap.
I was watching *Spiderman* on TV,
     cross-legged on the carpet
     wearing scuffed-up sneakers –
laces undone, feet sticky inside them.

I was eight by then,
a year after that first call which had turned
     everything
     inside out.

Mom shouted at me, as she always did.
'Turn the goddamn TV down!'

She had her cell to her ear,
was squinting like she was trying to see
whatever it was she was being told.

And then,
     like a rock into a river,
     she fell
     and began to howl.

It wasn't like you see in movies,
someone collapsing but so beautiful
　　　and
　　　tragic.
She was a person possessed,
smashing into pieces,
and I was afraid to get too close.
'No!' she screamed.

I knew right away the words she was hearing.
Anyone could have guessed.

We were kind of expecting it.

And not expecting it at all.

Aunt Karen had been at some of the short trial,
came home and
told us things weren't going Ed's way –
for starters, there was his confession
　　　the day after he got arrested.
She said that if she'd been on the jury,
she'd have locked him up and
　　　thrown away the key herself.

'He didn't do it,' Angela told her.

'I don't know any more,' Aunt Karen said.
'He looked pretty guilty to me.'

And the day that second call came,
I was the only other person at home,
alone again with Mom in the house
and
I didn't know what to do.
I mean,
Mom was always freaking out, but not like that:
      an animal caught in wire.

I went to her,
      tried to get her to stand,
      but
      she wouldn't.
      She couldn't.

      Mom stayed
      down for a
      really
      long
      time.

17

AUNT KAREN

Three hours after the bad news
our Aunt Karen came to stay.
'I'm all you've got,' she told us.

She stared at the ketchup stains on my white T-shirt,
like that was proof our family
couldn't take care of itself.
I wiped my nose with the back of my hand
and she flinched.

'We don't have space,' Angela explained.

Aunt Karen scratched her nose with her
thumbnail.
'I'll take your room. You can share with Joe
for a while.
Ed's old bed is still in there.'

Angela stood up as tall as she could.
'I need my privacy,' she said.

'Yeah, well,' Mom mumbled, cradling a gin.

'But I have exams,' Angela tried again.

'I know you do,' Aunt Karen said.
'And you'll pass them. I won't have you go down
the same road as Ed.'

It didn't matter how hard we stamped our feet,
Aunt Karen had made up her mind
and Mom was in no state to argue:
Aunt Karen was staying and
we would start going to church,
not just on Sundays but after school too.
TV was
    out
and Bible study was
    in.
Karen knew how to save our souls
from falling into the darkness
that had carried off our brother,
and the first part of her plan was
            to never mention Ed again.

Mom stopped going out.
    She littered the house with empty pill bottles.
    She watched infomercials,
    shopped through the TV,
    said she was waiting until people forgot,
    that she'd get her act together and
    go back to work
    once the worst blew over.

But

    she never returned to work and
    when she finally ventured out,

    she didn't come back.

AUTO SHOP

When I told Reed's uncle at the auto shop last week
that I was headed to Texas for the whole summer,
he didn't take it well either.
'I don't know if I can keep your job open, Joe,'
he said.
'I got guys queuing up to apprentice here
and you're taking off?'

I hadn't explained to anyone apart from Reed
the real reason I'd be gone.
I was ashamed and Reed must have guessed it.
'Give him a break, Uncle Sammy.
        Joe's got some girl knocked up
        and needs to get out of Arlington
        before her brothers do him in,' Reed said.

Sammy rubbed his greasy hands against
his blue overalls and frowned.
        'You're lyin'.'

        'He's lyin',' I said.
                'But I gotta go.
        I'll be back though.'

21

Sammy sighed. 'OK. OK.
You're a hell of a lot better than
Reed at getting dirty under a hood
anyway,
I'll give you that.'

Reed grunted and reached for a wrench.
'I prefer to get dirty in other ways.'

Sammy watched me.
'You're still standing there, Joe.
What do you want?'

I didn't like to ask.
It felt like begging.
'I'm owed two weekends.'

Reed snickered.

Sammy rolled his eyes, reached into
his pocket and pulled out a roll
of twenties.
'How much?' he asked.

TEAM WRONG

Back at the motel, I call Angela.
Her voice is high pitched and
something is buzzing in the background.
'I can't hear you, Ange!' I shout.

The buzzing stops.

'I'm at the bar making mojitos,' she says. 'You OK?'

I want to tell the truth, say,
No, I'm not OK.
It's hot.
I haven't any more money for food.
I'm solo doing this,
which isn't how it should be.
I'm seventeen years old, for Christ's sake.
Why aren't you here?
Why isn't Aunt Karen? Mom?

'I found an apartment,' I say,
leaving out the bit about the bugs.
'Will the cash have cleared in my account yet?'

She coughs into the phone.
'Should have,' she says.
'But then that's it.
The boss won't give me an advance
so it'll be next month before I've got
cash to come down there.'

'Aunt Karen?' I ask hopefully.

'No way. She's still super pissed.
She picked up more stuff,
said she isn't moving back in.
I don't even know how we'll make the rent
unless she changes her mind.
And how the hell are you gonna eat?'

'I'm looking for work.'

'I wish I could get more cash, Joe.'

I half-laugh.
            How exactly?
            Ask strangers for handouts?
We could never get away with that –
begging for loans to be with our brother.

See, we aren't the people anyone pities.
No one cares whether or not we get to be with
Ed at the end,
how poor or hungry we are.
The cop's widow though?

    If she set up a crowd-funding account
    to buy a black dress and matching hat,
    you'd have people donating
    big time.

            The widow of a murdered guy?
            Do you take Mastercard?

But we aren't her — we're not the victims here.

Instead we're on the other side of right —
            players for Team Wrong.

'Have you seen Ed?' Angela whispers.

I go to the bathroom,
run cold water into the shower.
'No,' I admit.

I haven't even tried.

CHICKEN SHIT

Ed wrote to me last month
asking for help.
I'm the one he thought he could rely on.

He probably imagined his baby brother
had grown into a
     man.

But I'm too chicken shit
to even call the prison
and enquire about visits,
let alone
        drag my sorry ass
up to the gates
and try to get in.

LETTER FROM ED

Hey Joe,

How you doing man?
You best be studying hard or I'll kick your ass!
> *Nah, I'm just playing.*

Thing is,
> *I didn't write Angela this week.*
> *Tell her it's my bad,*
> *but*
> *I need you to break something to her.*

> *I got my date through.*
> *Guys here telling me it's nothing to panic about.*
> *Just a date.*
> *But if I'm honest*
> *it makes me rattle like old bones,*
> *cos it means they*
> *made up their minds*
> *and wanna do me in.*
> *And for what?*
> > *For nothing.*
> > *For something I never did.*

The date they settled on is August 18, Joe,
but I got another appeal to go in the state courts
before then
and
we could go to federal for a couple more
I think.
Also there's a chance the governor will stop it
(or the president!)
so August 18's what they're planning on —
but if I convince them of the truth,
it might come and go
and I'll still be standing, you know.

Thing is,
I got no lawyer to advise me
and explain how everything works,
cos the state don't pay for lawyers until
eternity, right?
Anyway the prison's priest is doing
some detective work
and finding out what's what for me.

Thing is,
I'm wondering if you could come visit.
Father Matthew says that even though
you're not eighteen

they might let you come if Angela can't,
on special request.
I wrote the warden, and I'm waiting to hear.
In the nine years I been locked up in Wakeling
I only seen him a handful of times on the row.
No one comes down to see
us deadbeats unless they have to, I guess.
But
he seems like a regular kind of guy.
Worth asking.

Anyway,
I'll mail this now and write again when I know more.
Don't freak out, OK?
Let me do the sweating.
I got plenty of time for it.

Be cool, little brother,
Ed x

WHAT IT MEANT

I got that letter two weeks ago,
read it
then
threw it on the floor.

I couldn't touch it.
  Those words.
  What they meant.
  What I *guessed* they meant,
cos even Ed didn't seem too sure.

I was standing in my bedroom and
when I looked up
  Angela was in the doorway,
   purse under her arm.
She pointed at the rug,
the letter lying
   face up,
Ed's scrawl all over it.
'How is he?' she asked.

I wanted to tell her everything
but couldn't figure out what I knew.
'He's busy,' I said,

which was stupid – he's in prison –
how busy could it get?

'Did he like my card?'
                    She smiled,
                    scratched her belly.

'He didn't mention it.'
But he did mention an execution date.
He said I shouldn't worry,
but for the first time in ten years
Ed asked to see me,
sort of said he needed me,
which he'd never done before –
he'd always known the deal with Karen,
didn't want to mess up
things for Angela or me in Arlington.
'You guys get on with your lives,'
he said in a letter once.
So we tried.
We tried really hard to pretend Ed was OK –
that his death sentence was mythical
and not something that would ever really happen.

I closed my eyes. Rubbed my face.
'What time did you get in last night?' Angela asked.

'About one,' Karen snapped, appearing behind her.
'If you want to graduate next year, Joe,
you have to study.
Where were you?'

'The year's almost over, Karen,' I told her.
I wasn't going to admit I was with Reed,
smoking weed,
figuring out how to cheat on our Spanish test
the next day instead
of just studying for it.

I closed the door on both of them and
picked up the letter.
          I read it again just to be sure.

And I was.

It was true:
my only brother would be dead within two months,
and there was
                    nothing
I could say or
          do to
          stop it.

A DECISION

When I finally told Angela,
she shook and twitched,
wouldn't eat the eggs I'd scrambled.

She said she'd go to the bank
for a loan, get him a lawyer,
said she wanted to go down to Wakeling
to help.

But then Aunt Karen got home
from her night shift at the hospital
and tried to shake sense into my sister.
'There's nothing you can do,
and I won't have you
wasting your money or your life
fighting for someone
who's not even sorry.'

'Without a lawyer, he has no chance,' Angela argued.

'That isn't our fault,' Aunt Karen snapped back.

'He's my *brother*.'

'But not a good one.'

      I stood between them.
      '*I'm* going to Wakeling,' I announced,
      not knowing before the words
      were out
      whether or not I really wanted to see Ed.

But someone has to be here.

Angela's got a full-time job,
Aunt Karen hates him,
and no one knows where the hell Mom is.

That was decided two weeks ago
and nothing's changed except one thing:
Ed now has even less time to live.

MUGSHOT

The only TV channel in the motel that isn't pure static
is the early morning local news.
I watch the muted screen,
pulling on my sneakers,
when Ed's mugshot pops up.

He looks mean:
       chin raised,
       eyes small,
       face bruised.

I stare,
       scared.

What if Ed's like the guy
in that mugshot
and my memories of him aren't real at all?

And then his picture vanishes
and photos of Frank Pheelan flash up –
blue-eyed on a beach somewhere,
sand in his toes,
another of him in police uniform,
and then a family portrait with his wife and kids,

strawberry blonds, all of them,
with ripening smiles.
I've seen these faces before:
newscasters love revealing the beauty of the victims –
like they're the only ones who got slammed.

Reporters don't give a damn about our family.
We're not a story. We're dirt.
Although,
I guess that's a lot easier than having to admit
that by killing our brother
they're just pummelling more people.

The feature about Ed's looming execution ends
and a weather map replaces it.
Texas is covered in blazing yellow suns.

I lace up my sneakers;
        I'm going for a run regardless.

MORNING RUN

The traffic lights click and change,
though Wakeling's streets are still mostly empty of cars.

I run fast,
measuring my splits on my watch.
        I'm slower than usual.

I run and run,
try to get my speed up
and don't see anyone, which
is exactly why I go out first thing –
        for the quiet,
            the feeling of being the only person alive.

I pound the sidewalks,
my heart beating a million miles an hour,
and all I can focus on is breathing,
on not keeling over.

Which suits me.

Suits me just fine.

IN WALMART

Mr Porter stopped me in Walmart.
He had his son in the cart,
　　　　brown goo around the kid's mouth.
'Joe.
I saw Reed last night at training.
He told me you ain't going to the track and field
summer programme
in the city.'

'No, sir. I can't.'

He bit the insides of his cheeks.
'I had to apply for funding for the programme.
You didn't get the place by accident.'
His kid stood up in the cart,
tried to climb over the side
　　　　and make an escape.
Mr Porter pulled him out, let the boy
waddle up the cereal aisle.

'Something came up, sir. I'm sorry.'

'And you've missed a week of training.
I'm kind of disappointed.

You know my thoughts on your performances.
But I can't force anyone to want something
and talent isn't enough.
You have to work hard.'

I'd come into the store for toothpaste.
I hadn't planned on getting grilled
by a schoolteacher.
He meant well, but it was summer vacation –
he'd no right to nag me.

'I gotta go, sir,' I said.

'Is something going on?' he asked.

'Nah. Everything's cool,' I said.

I don't want anyone's pity.

HOME SWEET HOME

The landlord kicks a pile of junk mail
from the doormat,
leads the way into the kitchen and
rips opens the envelope I've handed him.
He counts out the cash and
holds a fifty dollar bill to the light.
Flies hum around us.
'No late check-outs. You got that?'
He dangles the keys in front of me.
I snatch them and he sucks on his teeth.
'What are you in Wakeling for anyway?
You know someone at the farm?'

I turn on the cold faucet.
Yellow water dribbles on to the mouldy dishes
piled up
       then abandoned
       by the previous tenant.

He shuts off the water.
'It'll run clear in a couple minutes.'
He glances around like he might have forgotten
       something,
then takes off,
slamming the door behind him.

I flick a switch.
Nothing happens.

I try another.
        No light.

I dart to the door,
        holler into the hallway.
'The electricity is out! Hey, there's no light!'

        But I'm alone
        and the hallway
        is in darkness too.

LITTLE MURDERS

I murder close to twenty cockroaches
with the base of a rusty pan.
Their backs crack and crunch.
'Dirty bastards.'

The apartment smells worse than I remember,
like whoever lived here
let their cat
or kid
piss all over the carpets.

In the living room
            I try opening a window
            but it's painted shut.
Grime and grease cake the pane.

I check my phone.
No one's messaged or called since yesterday.
Not Reed, Karen, not even Angela,
which is sort of surprising and a bit shitty.
Do they think I'm here
soaking up sun and scratching my ass?

I'm here for Ed. That's it.

I'm here cos he's my blood.
He needs me.
It's what I have to do.
But if I had a choice?
I'd be on a plane home –
        I'd be gone.

A single roach scuttles out from
        underneath the spongy sofa.
I stamp on it,
then look up
and realise
the damn things are crawling
        the walls.

NO REPLY

I message Reed:
> Hot as hell here, man!
> SHIIIIIT! Wots happenin????

After a moment
I see he's read the message.
I watch my screen, wait for his smartass reply.
But nothing comes through, and then
he's offline.

> So I put my phone into my
> back pocket and
> head out.

STAR WARS

We used to play on the sidewalk,
brandishing long sticks as lightsabers,
caning one another and
really feeling the force of it.

Then Ed got a real lightsaber,
gave it to me grinning.
'*Join me*,' he said,
Darth Vader croaky.
But the dark side
never really appealed to me,
so I lit up my green sword
and used it to
        slice him
        to pieces.
He groaned, rolled on the ground,
while the kids in the neighbourhood watched,
jealous for a brother like mine.

We watched *Stars Wars* obsessively,
and during a bad storm,
when school closed,
saw every movie back to back,

only stopping
to grab bags of chips for nourishment.

'Can't we watch *anything* else?' Angela groaned.

Ed turned to her, horrified.
'I feel like we shouldn't be family any more.'
He threw a pillow at her
and she laughed,
slumped on the couch next to us.
'Seriously, Ange, you're missing out.'

'Angela doesn't like fighting,' I said
to defend my sister,
and Ed nodded sympathetically,
then sucked on the back of his hand.
'Yeah. She prefers kissing.'

Angela covered her eyes with her forearm.
'You're grossing me out.
That must be how *you* kiss your girlfriends.'

We were creased up but hushed as
Mom slithered into the sitting room.

'I'm ordering takeout,' she said.
Her eyes were black-rimmed,
sweatpants and hoodie creased.
She coughed and coughed
until she had to leave the room,
then called in from the kitchen.
'Angela, can you phone for pizza?
My voice is cut to crap.'

'Sure, Mom!' Angela said,
her tone like sunshine,
as though Mom wasn't a complete screw-up.

'Can we get plain cheese?' I asked.

'Course we can, little man,' Ed said, pulling me close,
turning up the TV.
R2-D2 slid across a spaceship.

Angela dialled for dinner
and we watched *Star Wars*
into the night
while Mom threw up in the bathroom.

She said she had a bug,
told us not to come close
in case we caught what she had.

And even though none of us bought the bug story,
we all kept out of Mom's way.

WHEN THE COP GOT SHOT

After the first call came through from Ed,
Angela tried to explain
what he had been accused of
and what might happen next.
But I never really got my head around it.

When kids in my class asked
for the details
I couldn't think what to say.
Ed had taken off months before,
right after his big bust-up with Mom.
I had no idea where he was
the day Frank Pheelan got shot.

The day it happened
I was on a field trip to
the Liberty Science Center,
eating a bologna sandwich,
thinking about space,
Mars mostly,
a planet so close, so completely inhospitable.
I wasn't thinking about cops or death.

And until Angela explained it,
I didn't know that to be accused of murder
in the wrong state was
                fatal.

ICE AND FLAME

Aunt Karen took me into New York City
the Christmas after Ed was convicted
so we could skate in Central Park,
something I hadn't done before.
She held my mittened hand,
stopped me slipping on the ice.
All I was thinking was
how much
funnier the trip would have been with Ed.
He'd have made Karen lighten up, laugh,
instead of worrying about
the other skaters' blades
chopping off our fingers if we fell.

Afterwards we walked down Fifth Avenue
to St Patrick's Cathedral
where Karen lit red candles,
and in front of the tiny flickering flames,
prayed for our family on her knees.
I lit a candle for Ed,
thought about him alone during the holidays
in a cell with no tinsel or twinkling lights,

no chance of seeing a full moon
or any moon
for that matter.

'Did you pray?' Aunt Karen asked on our
          way out,
dipping her fingers into the stone font
and crossing herself with holy water.

In the street I admitted,
'I prayed for the cops to send Ed home.'

Karen knelt again, in the middle of the sidewalk,
this time to look me straight in the eye.
'I've read the reports and spoken to the lawyers, Joe.
Forget about Ed.
He isn't ever coming home, OK?
Ever.'

People nudged me with the corners of their
fancy shopping bags.
'He told me he didn't do it,' I said.

'He's lying,' she said.

'*You're* lying,' I never said.

Instead I decided right then
never to defend Ed again,
and
let my aunt
believe I didn't love him any more.

MIRACLES

Sue is outside Bob's Diner,
    smoking and
      blinking at the sun.
'You're here,' she says.
'I thought you was full of bullcrap.'

'Where's the car?' I ask.

She uses her hand as a visor,
looks me up and down.
'You gonna fix it with superpowers, hun?'

I lift my baseball cap,
scratch the hair beneath it –
I hadn't thought about tools.

Sue snickers.
'Bob don't got a needle and thread,
but lucky for you
I borrowed my Lenny's toolbox.
He sees something missing, I'm for it,
so you give it back how you found it, right?'
She wags a bejewelled finger at me.

54

'You'll also need a miracle,
but Lenny didn't have none of those.
You looking for a miracle, hun?'

I shrug.
        Try to look tough.

'Who's at the farm?' she asks.

'Huh?'
First the landlord, now her?
Is it written on my face?

She sucks deeply on the cigarette.
'Look, no one shows up round here
unless they got business at the farm.'

I hesitate. Do I trust her?
Even if I don't,
        I can't keep Ed a secret for long –
not in a town this size.
'My brother's down to die next month.'

Sue raises her eyebrows.
'And you're in Texas alone?'

'I don't mind,' I lie.
　　　　　　I kick the dirt.

'Is he guilty?' she asks.

What am I supposed to say?
Well, Ed says he isn't
and he's never lied to me before
but who knows?
Guys on the row must lie all the time.

She drops the glowing butt of her cigarette,
grinds it into the ground
with the heel of her rubber-soled shoe.
'You want a hot breakfast, hun?'

I nod.

Why the hell is she being so nice?
She doesn't know me and
what she *does* know is the bad stuff —
the stuff I usually keep to myself.

'Junker's open out back. Good luck.'

THE FARM

When dogs get put down
parents tell their kids
the mutts got sent to a farm
to live out their last days
with peppy ducks and rabbits.

And it's as though the state of Texas thinks
we're all just as stupid as kids,
calling the state penitentiary
          'Wakeling Farm' –
like inmates lie around on hay bales
and spend their afternoons milking cows.

But just like the dogs,
most guys who go to this farm
don't ever come home.

THE JUNKER

It really is a junker:
dried out grass growing around the wheels;
hubcaps gone or stolen;
the hood infected with rusty scabs;
not a dribble of oil in the clapped-out engine;
no gas in the tank.

I've no idea where to start.

But if I want to eat,
I've got to get this crap heap running.

Soon.

INSIDE OUT

When Ed got his driver's licence
Aunt Karen acted like he'd made honour roll.
'Look at you! Driving!
Soon you'll be married
and how old will that make me?'
She smacked him playfully.

Ed grinned.
'Ah, Karen, you got good genes.
You're gonna outlive us all.
Anyway, it's about time …
          I should've got my licence last year.'

Angela looked up from her book.
'He's being cute cos he wants your wheels, Aunt Karen.'

'What? That's real suspicious of you, Angela,' Ed said.
'But … if our very cool aunt wants to lend me her car,
I won't say no.'
He jabbed at Karen's coat pocket.
Keys clinked.

She backed away.
'Oh no. Borrow someone else's car.'

Karen was tough, but that day
        Ed was persistent;
        he spent twenty minutes
        wearing her down
        until she handed over the keys
        to her twelve-year-old Mitsubishi.
'Be *careful*,' she pleaded.

Ed said,
'I won't go over a hundred, I promise,'
and wrapped his arm around my shoulder.
He smelled of spicy deodorant and spearmint gum.
'You coming, co-pilot?'

Aunt Karen slumped on the sofa next to Angela,
who put down her book and
        pushed her feet into a pair of purple Converse.
'I'll go with them, Aunt Karen.'
She turned on the T.V.
'You enjoy *Ellen*. We'll be back soon.'

'Where's your mom?' Karen asked.

'Work,' Angela said,
when we all knew she was probably at a bar
or with some guy she'd just met.

Ed was in charge of the driving,
Angela of the music,
and I was in the back seat feeding them snacks
after we'd stopped at a bodega and
bought a whole bag of candy.

'No *way*,' Ed groaned, as Angela turned the radio
to a station playing pop.

'Oh, what would you prefer, DJ Badass?'

'Anything, dude. *Anything.*'

Angela fiddled with the dials, then stopped.

'Elvis!' Ed cheered.
        'Jesus,' Angela said.
'The King,' Ed replied. 'Turn it up!'
        'Oh, come on, Ed.
        Want a blanket for your knees too?'
He smacked the steering wheel.
'Turn it *up*!'

And   she did.
And   the windows were down.
And   Ed was singing.
And   then Angela was singing.
And   the song wasn't too difficult to learn.
And   I started singing.

After Elvis
it was Johnny Cash,
then The Supremes
and more singers and songs that I didn't know
but I sang along anyway,
          screeching out the windows
                    as we boomed along Third Avenue.

Aunt Karen was waiting on the stoop,
wringing her hands on a dishcloth.

Angela turned off the music.
'Cool drive. Thanks, Ed,' she said
and jumped out of the car,
practically skipping into the house.

Ed sat speechless behind the wheel.

'You coming?' I asked.

'When you're my age, screw Driver's Ed.
I'm gonna teach you to drive.
And then you, me and Ange'll go for another ride.
Deal?'

'Deal,' I said.
      I climbed out,
      stood on the sidewalk.

He stayed where he was, staring out the
      windshield.

I knocked on the passenger window. 'Ed?'

He turned to me and winked.
'Tell Karen I've gone to get milk,' he said, and
pulled away again slowly.

Karen squealed. I smirked.
But while we waited for him to return
I got to thinking,
even way back then

when I was too young to understand much:
you can know all the facts you want about
            a person
– height, weight, the way they like their eggs –
but you'll never know for sure what's
            driving his heart.

ED NEVER CAME BACK

Ed didn't return with the milk
or Aunt Karen's car.
We waited all evening, night,
     the next day
           and the rest of the week,
but by Sunday
it was clear –
        he was gone.

'You owe me the cost of a car,' Aunt Karen told Mom.

'It's your own fault – you gave him the keys.
I wouldn't trust Ed with a toothbrush.'

They argued.
Screamed and shouted,
     Mom swearing at the top of her lungs
that she was fed up with the whole damn lot of us,
Aunt Karen storming home,
riding the bus since she'd nothing to drive.

'You won't go too, will you?' I asked Angela,
tucked up next to her in an armchair,
eating nachos.

'Don't worry,' she told me.
'Everything's gonna blow over,
go back to normal.
        You'll see.'

But since when had our family been 'normal'?

Since
        never.

WHY HE LEFT ...

I was in the next room making a space rocket from
two cardboard boxes Ed had brought home.
Their voices came through from the kitchen,
quiet at first then louder and louder
until I couldn't ignore them.

'You forgot to get bread for Joe's lunch,' Ed said.
'So go to the store. You have money,' Mom told him.
'Yeah, but I'm not his parent.'
'Well, no, but you sure as hell act like mine.'

Silence.

'You know,
        it's about time you got your own place,'
Mom said.
'You're kicking me out?' Ed asked.
'You're like your father,
        and he wasn't very likeable.'
'Well, thank God I'm not like *you*.'
'Excuse me?'
'Oh, come on, Mom. Look at you. You're a joke.'
'What?'

'A. Joke. Everyone knows it. Even Joe.'
'Take that back.'
'No. You're either drunk or hung-over.'
'So get out.'
'No.'
'I said get out! It's my house.'

More silence.
A smack.
> Ed tumbled out of the kitchen,
> one cheek
> flashing pink.

'I can't take this any more,' he said.

It was a few days later that
> he took off in Karen's car.

NELL

'For you. From Sue,' a voice says,
making me jump.
I knock my head against the hood and
drop the car battery.

A girl is standing with a
          tray balanced between two hands.
She places a plate of eggs, a bottle of water,
on the roof of the car,
pulls a plastic fork from the
          pocket of her apron,
          hands it to me.
She's wearing a bowling shirt like Sue's,
the name *Nell* embroidered in black.

She turns and struts off.
          But I don't want her to leave.
I want to talk to someone,
have a regular conversation
where I'm not begging for something or
having to explain what I'm doing here.
'You work at the diner?'
It's the only question I've got.

She stops. Turns.
'Do you have an above average IQ?
You're *very* sharp.
You should be on a game show.'

I call out.
'Wanna share my water?'
I hold it aloft,
jiggle it about,
try to be funny,
pretty sure I look and sound like an idiot.

She grins.
'I hear that stuff can kill you.'
She marches off.
The laces of her sneakers trail on the ground;
her hair is tied haphazardly on top of her head
        and wobbles when she walks.

I'm about to shout again,
a third-time-lucky kind of thing,
but don't.
Sweat has pooled at the base of my back,
my head hammers from the heat.
I need to eat.

Still standing,
I gorge on the almost-cold scrambled eggs
in a few greedy bites,
guzzle down the water too,
and I'm about to get back to rooting around
        under the hood
when my phone rings.

A PRIZE

'Al Mitchell here. Is that Joe?'
Ed's lawyer sounds breezy,
not at all as serious as I'd imagined he would be,
and for a second I wonder
if Ed is
        off the hook,
if we can fly back to New York together and
pretend none of this happened.
I know we'll never be the Waltons,
but maybe we could be a messed-up family again.

'Hello, Mr Mitchell,' I say.

'Nice to speak to you finally, Joe.
Angela's told me a lot about you.
I've already called her.
I have good news.'

        He pauses.
        Takes a breath.
        And I do too.

'We got you full visitation rights to the row, Joe.
The warden's secretary called my office,

said you can visit today.
And every day after that at two.'

I don't reply.
This is good news?
That I can see my brother,
talk about girls and cook-outs,
do my best to haul his mind
away from the truth?

This isn't something to celebrate:
this is just bad news turned upside down,
bad news inflated and painted
to twinkle like a prize.

'I've lost you, Joe,' Mr Mitchell says.
'I think the connection's bad.'

'Thank you,' I say.
And then, 'I'll visit this afternoon.'

The lawyer detects my disappointment,
tries again.
'We still have one round left at state level.
Then we've got the US Supreme Court
and the governor.

I believe we can do this.
It's not the end.
We save men all the time.
Oh,
        and Joe?'

'Yeah?'

'Please call me Al.'

THE CHECKLIST

I look for a scrap of paper and the nub of a pencil
on the back seat of the car
so I can
scribble down
the three parts of the process left:
    the state court,
    the Supreme Court,
    the governor.
I want to remember
what we are waiting for,
what to expect.
But I can't find anything to write with.
And I guess it's unlikely I'll forget
Ed's three slim chances
of getting out of here.

POOR JUSTICE

Ed didn't have a lawyer for years.
After a few rounds in court
he was no longer entitled to a public defender
and we couldn't afford to pay anyone
   to represent him.

Ed was just left in Texas to rot
and we didn't know what to do about it.

Wasn't until he got his date through
that Angela wrote to every non-profit
in the country
and eventually found Al Mitchell,
   who agreed to take on the case
   for free
   as charity.

And for the first time someone listened
and
made us think a different outcome was possible.

Al also explained to Angela
that most guys on the row don't have a lawyer
and

spend half their time
begging for representation
or
studying the law themselves.
'Like your brother did,' he'd told her,
though we hadn't known Ed
was educating himself in the law from his cell.

'God. It's better to be guilty and rich,
          I reckon,' I'd told Angela.
It was a couple of nights before I flew down to Texas.
We were eating noodles from boxes.

'No doubt!' Angela agreed.
'But now we've got Al, we've got hope.
He said the whole case was based on bullshit.'

I chewed on chow mein
but didn't respond.
Hope wasn't really
          my area of expertise.

DISTRACTION

I poke and pull at the car,
hands plastered in oil,
and don't stop until one o'clock,
when the sun has cooked me through.

Then I take off without telling anyone.

I don't want to go to the prison.

But I can't be late either.

WHO IS EDWARD MOON?

A text comes through from Aunt Karen:
> A lawyer by the name of
> Alan Mitchell called.
> Said you're visiting Ed today.
> Are you sure about this, Joe?

And of course the answer is
> no.

I mean, who the hell is Edward Moon?
He was my brother
> but I hardly know him now.

Last time I saw him I was seven years old.
What if I don't like him?
And he might hate me.
We could sit there gaping,
wondering what the fuck to discuss and
counting down every awkward minute,
a bit like those parent–teacher conferences
where everyone is so frickin' polite
and you can't even make eye contact
with a person who's been teaching
you every day for two semesters.

I'm not sure about any of this.
But I'm here now.

> And seeing Ed
> is why I've come.

PARENT-TEACHER CONFERENCE

Ed showed up for my parent–teacher conference in
ripped jeans.
I sat opposite my first grade teacher,
watched her features as she yabbered,
noted Ed listening,
wondered how much he understood
cos I couldn't follow any of it:
tardiness, attainment, literacy.

Afterwards
Ed conjured up a candy bar from his denim jacket.
'I swiped that, so please enjoy,' he said,
not a hint of shame,
maybe even a slice of pride.
He never usually admitted to stealing stuff
even though I knew he couldn't afford
the sneakers he wore
or the phone he used.

At home,
Mom was in bed.
'It was parent–teacher night,' Ed explained
from her bedroom doorway.

She groaned.
'God, I forgot. Do they think you'll graduate?'

'It was *mine*,' I corrected her.

                                        Ed walked away.

Mom pulled back her blanket,
gestured for me to join her.

'I have homework,' I lied.

Mom didn't protest. 'Close the door.'

My hands were coated in candy bar chocolate and
Ed stood behind me while
I washed them in the basin,
one hand on my shoulder.

'Mom cares more than she shows,' he said.

'Does she?' I asked.

I was six.

Six years old, still wetting the bed,
no parent to walk me to school
or
make my bagged lunch.

And even then
I knew better
than to believe him.

SECTION A

'The row's apart from the rest of the prison,'
a guard says,

        leading me out of the main building
        into the heat.
He points the way to Section A
    where Ed's
    locked up with the other death row inmates,
    the damned safely separated
    from the merely bad.

The Section A office is smaller, stuffier,
grey walls instead of green.
A massive guard, built like a marine,
    looks up
    from his desk.

'I'm here to see Edward Moon,' I say.

He stands slowly, sighing,
palm against his lower back.
'You're the brother.'

'Yeah. Joseph Moon.'
I feel really young suddenly,

like I'm about to get grilled by the principal,
like I'm here cos I've done something dishonest myself.

'ID,' he says.

I hand over my driver's licence
and he points to my backpack.
'No bags.'

I open the top pocket,
          take out a bottle of water.

The guard shakes his head.
'Did you read the conditions of visitation?'
He licks his lips,
surprises me by speaking softly.
'Got anything else, son? Penknife? Recording device?'
I hand over my phone and
he crams everything into a locker,
gives me a ticket like a cloakroom clerk and says,
'This way.'

I'm led through a
                    sliding door,

a floor-to-ceiling metal gate
then
another entryway
that squeals as it
     opens,
     clangs as it
     shuts.
So many doors and bars, but no windows,
     not even high up,
     out of reach,
     to let natural daylight strain into the hall.
It's all fluorescent lighting,
flickering and humming,
like the building itself is

          strung out.

From somewhere close by comes a holler –
a laugh, barbed and desperate.

     The concrete walls press in on me,
     my chest tightens.

Another gate,
opened and closed –
     more clanging, crashing,
     slamming, squealing.

The marine-guard studies my expression.
'You'll get used to it. We all do,' he says,
like he could possibly know
how I feel.

I want to tell him to go
                suck it
                but
I think I might be sick.

I'm led
        along a hallway,
                a sign above it:
                DEATH ROW,
                words printed in sloping
                red capitals
                like a vicious warning.

'I can't let you see him if you're gonna lose it.
Understand?' the marine-guard asks.

'Yes,' I say,
understanding that despite
where I am and why I'm here,

I have to pretend I'm cool;
I have to pretend that visiting Ed
isn't making me feel like someone's
        grabbing,
                pulling at my guts with their
                bare hands.
Maybe I should whistle too.
Would that help everyone feel better?

He taps a ton of numbers into
a keypad on the wall
before elbowing open the final door –
the door to the
visiting room.

THE VISITING ROOM

A row of five booths,
hard chairs in each of them and
black telephones.

> The other side of the booth the same
> > and
> > separating them
> some pretty tough-looking Plexiglas.

There's no air con,
though it must be close to ninety degrees.
I think about asking for water,
but I won't take anything from these people.

Ever.

NOT A HOSPITAL

Everyone mouths off about
how much they hate the smell of hospitals,
but have any of them been to a prison?

IT'S ED

I don't look at the Plexiglas.
I study the floor,
my dusty sneakers,
then my hands, engine grease under the nails
to prove I haven't wasted my morning.

Something slams behind me.
      I don't turn.
I'm scared to look anywhere
      except
      down.

So I sit stiff in the chair.
I don't look at the Plexiglas.
I study the floor,
and finally a shadow
      falls.

      I look up.

      It's Ed.

COCO

The Ed I knew
didn't have the balls to kill a cat,
let alone a cop.

When our cat Coco got real sick
but the vet was out of town for the weekend,
Mom said, 'For Christ's sake, take that thing
down to the Hudson and do it a favour.'

Coco was cradled in his arms,
mewling like a newborn.
She couldn't move her own limbs,
hadn't eaten anything for days.
Her black fur was falling out.
        She was as light as a kitten.

Still, Ed held on.
'You want me to take Coco to the river and *drown* her?'

We were in the backyard.
Mom was smoking a cigarette.
Ed and I were playing 'I Spy'.
He wasn't letting me win;
he never did, just cos I was younger,
and I liked that.

'It would be the kindest thing to do,' Mom said.

'Since when have *you* cared about the kindest thing?'
he murmured,
not wanting to upset the cat.

Mom rose, pushed her chair back.
'That thing's a goner.
Only difference doing it on Monday will be that
Dr Death takes a hundred bucks off us
for the privilege of letting her suffer.
I've got a bag in the closet –
we could do it for free.'

Ed glanced at me, kept his voice low.
'I'm not putting Coco into a *fucking* bag.'

Mom slung
        her burning cigarette
        into the dry grass.
'I'll get someone else to do it. Give her here.'

Ed recoiled,
eyes blazing,
the muscles in his neck tightening.

'I'm not paying for the vet,' Mom insisted.

Coco mewled again,
thinner this time,
begging to be saved from our mother.

'Come on, Joe,' Ed said.
He marched into the house,
knocking Mom out of the way
as he charged through the
        back door.

In our room, Ed passed the cat to me and
spread out a fleece on his bed.
I flattened my face against her bony head and
she licked me with a gravelly tongue.
She hissed.
'Maybe it hurts to be held,' he suggested.
I put her down gently and Coco lay still,
                        closed her eyes.
'I'll go to the drug store and buy a baby bottle,
get her to drink some milk.'

I nodded.
'Do you think Coco might get better?' I asked.

'No, Joe. Coco's gonna die,' he said
with certainty.

'You think she knows that?'

'I sure as hell hope not.'
He grabbed his cell phone from his desk.
'Call me if Mom tries to touch her.'

I curled up on the bed next to Coco,
watched as her tiny body
        moved
        up and
        down
        with her shallow breath.
I wasn't one for praying but
I asked Jesus to save Coco,
stop her being eaten alive
from the inside by a massive tumour.

My prayer didn't work though,
and by morning,
when I woke up next to her,
Ed asleep in the other bed,
        Coco was cold.

THE PRISONER

White jumpsuit,
hair shaved close,
a bolt and crossbow tattooed on
one side
of his neck,
sloppily done, by another inmate maybe.

Ed smiles,
lips stretched thin,
revealing every bad tooth in his head.

And I smile back,
cos I'm not sure what else to do.

I was right to be nervous:
I don't know this person
shifting in his seat,
hunched like an old man,
a person in his own right
and not
just carefully constructed memories
and half-baked stories.

He's your brother, I tell myself.
He's your blood.
Be cool for fuck's sake.

Ed flexes his fingers.

Sure, he *is* my brother
but he's also a grown man
I haven't seen for more than a decade
with a whole life
that hasn't included me.

This Ed is a stranger.

MARINER'S MARSHES

He was loitering outside the school gates,
hood up,
coat zipped to his chin,
        looking shifty.
'Ed,' I said,
and skipped towards him.

I followed him up the street
and we walked and walked,
        finally reaching Mariner's Marshes
        about a mile away.
'We're not allowed to go in there,' I said,
        knowing the park had been
        closed off to the public since
        before I was born.

Ed grinned and took my hand,
        led me into a place very few
people in Staten Island dared to go –
        an industrial wasteland,
        a perfect wilderness,
a place filled with burnt-out cars,
old ship parts,
and dotted with ponds, marshes, swamps.

Every kid in the neighbourhood knew
that a guy called Dempsey Hawkins
brought his girlfriend here in the Seventies
and killed her.
              It's the perfect place for it –
              deserted, quiet,
              old barrels and tunnels
              where you could easily hide a body.

Ed led me to one of the yellow-bricked
passageways,
icicles clinging to the roof of the tunnel.
'Why are we here?' I asked.
Ed opened up his backpack,
took out a carton of milk
and handed it to me.
'I don't wanna go home yet.
I flunked out of school,' he said.

'Why?'

'Cos I'm a loser.'

I slurped milk through the straw.
It was so cold it made my brain ache.
'You're not a loser, Ed.'

'I gotta get outta Arlington.
I gotta get out
and make something of myself.'

I'd heard it before.
It was Ed's refrain –
>   *I gotta go,*
>   *I'm leaving,*
>   *I can't stay.*

'Will you be OK if I'm not around?' he asked.

'Sure,' I said,
but I didn't mean it.
Ed was my brother but also
sort of like
my dad
and my best friend too.

It grew dark and we stayed right where we were –
huddled together beneath the cloudless sky
and a full moon that rose slowly
and lit up the wilderness
with yellow light.

'It almost makes you gasp to look at it,' Ed said,
pointing to the sky.
'Or makes you want to hide.'

I put my head on his shoulder.
'I could come with you,' I said.
I always said this and Ed always agreed.

'Sure,' he replied,
and ruffled my hair.
'Definitely.'

THE FIRST VISIT

'He can't hear you, kid,' the marine-guard says
     as I start to speak.
     'Use the phone.'

I put the handset to my ear.
Ed does the same
once the guard has yanked off his handcuffs.
His breath whistles down the line.
'Jesus, man, you look thirty years old,' he says.
His voice is scratchy,
like he's spent the years smoking,
and doesn't sound like the home videos Angela's kept
or even the guy I spoke to on the phone
a couple years ago
when Karen was gone away for a few days.
No trace of an Arlington accent.

I run a hand through my hair.
'The puberty troll turned up.
Said she couldn't wait any longer and
gave me facial hair.
Bitch.'

Ed laughs, bangs the desk
     between us.

His guard glowers.
My marine clears his throat.

'So, how you getting on, Joe?'
        He leans forward to listen.
But what am I supposed to say?
I'd prefer to crack jokes for an hour
than talk about stuff that matters.
Then again, what *does* matter?

I sit up straighter.
'I'm doing good. Got an apartment
and if I can turn over a junker, I'll get a job too.'

He smiles. 'You're here for how long?'

I pause.
'For as long as you need me,' I say.

He raises an eyebrow.
'And you got an apartment?
Shit.
When I first came to Texas,
I loafed around for months.
Here half a second and got yourself set up?
You aren't like me, Joe, that's for sure.'

He rubs one eye with the heel of his hand,
holds the handset under his chin for a second.
'So ...' he says eventually.

'Yeah. So.'
I wait for him to say something
but he's struggling as much as I am.

'Are you ... Is your ...' I begin,
wondering about his case.
But before I've formed a question,
I change my mind,
ask something meaningless.
'How's the food?'

Ed sticks one finger into his mouth and
makes a gagging noise.
'It's lousy, man. Farm can't spend more than
a couple dollars on any meal,
so it's cheese and chunder most days.'
He pauses, embarrassed.
'Don't suppose you could stick a few bucks
into my account for snacks?
        I hate to ask.
I guess Karen decided to stop sending cash.
I did wonder when that would happen.'

'Karen was sending cash?'

'A few dollars a month, yeah.
Rarely answered letters though.
As I said, I hate to ask, but …'

I hold up a hand,
        stop him speaking.
'No problem,' I say, even though I've spent
my last dime on rent and haven't the fare for a
        bus ride back into town.

He sighs. 'How's Angela?'

I shrug.
'She's OK. Works a lot.'

He scratches his scalp,
starts to bite what's left of a thumbnail.
'She got her head around this?'

'She's got Karen,' I lie,
cos Ed still doesn't know
        our aunt left last week
        on account of me being here and
that Angela and I are pretty much
fending for ourselves.

In a flash, he brightens.
'So the job? You gonna be a drug dealer's wheels?'

I laugh,
and we talk about my running,
school,
the price of gas,
sports and
then *Star Wars*,
me trying to convince him that
Rey's way cooler than Princess Leia
ever was,
cos, of course, he hasn't seen the new ones.

It's all
unimportant things
and never
                    The Thing.

And then, time's up.

'Three o'clock,' the marine shouts
to no one in particular,
though I'm the only one in the room.

'I'll come tomorrow,' I tell Ed.

106

'Have you heard from Mom?'
     he asks quickly.

I haven't a chance to answer.

     Already they've grabbed the phone off him,
     shackled his wrists and ankles,
     and are roughly leading him away.

UP AGAINST A COOKIE JAR

Angela thought the note
     propped up
     against an empty cookie jar
     was a joke.
'Why would Mom go to Minnesota on a bus?'

I didn't understand either.
She was gone? Like never coming back?
Like Dad was dead and Ed was in prison?

Aunt Karen rushed out to work,
cursing Mom for making us worry.

Angela and I ditched school.
We watched TV, waited for Mom to call
or come home.

We thought by the time it got dark
she would stagger in
carting a stuffed-crust pizza.
Maybe she'd smell of beer or be
dozy from pills,
but that would be all right.

Better home
and
    out of it
than on a Greyhound to the Midwest.

Only it didn't happen.
Mom never came home
and Aunt Karen took over completely,
raging with Ed for what he'd done to us.

I was nine by then.

A week after Mom took off
we got a letter from Ed,
dropping on to the mat with a considered huff.
He wanted to know when we were heading
        down to Texas
        to see him.
'I wouldn't visit that lowlife
if he was tied to a tree in the yard,' Karen yelled.
'He destroyed this family.
He destroyed two families.'
She wasn't interested in his innocence.
Guilty by judge and jury was enough,
and she made sure we knew it.

'He killed a police officer
and finished off your mother.'

Mom didn't vanish entirely though.
She sent postcards sometimes.

I never bothered to keep them.

EVERYONE WALKED

I	never had a dad
but	I had a big brother
and	then I didn't
and	then I didn't have a mother
and	I spent a lot of time wondering
when	I would lose
my	sister
my	aunt,
until	everyone I loved walked out the front door

leaving me alone.

THE GAS STATION

The girl from the diner, Nell,
studies a display of DVDs
along the back wall of the gas station.
I move towards her,
open a packet of gum without paying for it.
'I met you earlier,' I say,
offering her a piece.

Nell's face is stony.
'You're new to town.'
It's not a question.
She takes the gum from my hands,
pops a piece into her mouth and
puts the packet into her pocket.
'Your dad at the farm for robbery? Drugs?'

'My brother. His name's Ed. I'm Joe.'

She holds up a copy of *Die Hard*.
'Bruce Willis used to be so hot.'
She prods his picture on the box,
            tilts her head to one side.

'But he's not hot now?' I ask.

'He might be.
I haven't seen him since the restraining order.'
Her mouth is straight – a wise-ass.

She takes the DVD to the counter,
pays,
leaves
and stomps through the gas station parking lot,
along the sidewalk
        to an empty bench.

I drop down next to her.
'So DVDs. Bruce Willis. What else?'

She considers this.
'I just think old stuff is underrated.
Like Cyndi Lauper.
She's awesome.
Why the hell isn't she on the radio *all* the time?'

'Cyndi Lauper?' I snicker.

'Yeah, Cyndi Lauper.
And Dusty Springfield.
Do you even know Dusty Springfield?'

'Oh, sure, Dusty and I go *way* back.'
I wink at her but her expression is unreadable.
I struggle to find something else to say.
'You wanna grab some pizza?' I ask.

She waves the DVD case in my face.
'I've a date with Bruce.'

I'm not sure I like her,
but after the day I've had, I don't wanna be alone,
not for a third consecutive evening
with a bag of chips, my phone and the internet;
that sort of night can only go one way.
'Hang with me for an hour,' I beg.

'You might be a murderer,' she says.

'Do murderers take their victims for pizza?'

'*You'd* know.'

I swallow hard. Maybe I do know.
Maybe murderers look like the rest of us.
Maybe one looks a lot like me.

'You know, when I said let's go for pizza,
I meant would you buy me pizza cos I'm broke.'

'You must be if you can't afford gum,' she says.
So she noticed.

I wink at her again, hoping she'll find me
cute, not criminal.
She doesn't give anything away,
puts her hand into the pocket of her denim shorts,
pulls out some crumpled dollar bills.
'Don't go spending that on liquor and loose women.'

    I push her hand away.
    Yes, I'm starving,
    but for conversation.
    I want to talk to her,
    forget why I'm in Wakeling,
    be seventeen instead of a grown-up –
    serious and sensible.
    And hell, if I make her laugh
    maybe she'll let me kiss her,
    help me forget everything
    for a while.

Her phone beeps.

'I have to go.'

Across the street, a truck mounts the kerb.

'Enjoy the pizza.'

She throws the cash on to the bench.

'And wear something revealing next time.'

I laugh. And it's real.

'I'll dig out my purple hot pants,' I say.

She smirks. 'I'm Nell, by the way.'

'What sort of stalker would I be

if I didn't already know that?'

She nods, smiles and

rushes off to meet the waiting truck.

SCRATCH CARD

I should put the pity-cash Nell gave me
into Ed's account
so he can get a snack.

I don't.
I return to the gas station,
buy a scratch card,
take it back to the apartment and
scrape away silver foil
      with the edge of a dime.

I think about Nell in her shorts and baggy T-shirt,
not Ed in his jumpsuit.

I try really hard not to think about Ed.

And I don't beat the odds:
no matching numbers
beneath the panel of clover.

I think of Nell.
I think of her
      and I scratch.

UNLUCKY FOR SOME

Ed was convicted of shooting a cop,
a pretty ugly thing to do.
But you don't see every killer getting the gurney.
Some guys get fifteen years,
          others get life.

So death for Ed
but not for everyone.

Cos it all depends on
who you kill
and
where you kill them
too.

Like,
don't shoot a white cop in Walker County, Texas.
If that's your plan, do it in Arlington, New York –
no needles or electric chairs there.

Just doesn't seem fair to me.

Just seems a bit fucking random.

GOLD

Reed sends me a photo of the glossy gold medal
he's won for the steeple chase.
He gets a medal every year
even though hundreds of city kids do the
programme,
but he rarely comes first —
that's my job:
      gold for the five thousand metres.

      Just not this year.

Congrats, man!!!!!
I reply.
But I'm not noble enough
to be genuinely pleased.

A DIFFERENCE

Ed waves widely – Ronald McDonald style.
'Did Al call you today?'
He's almost bouncing in his chair.

I shake my head
    but my body
    lightens,
    untightens.
Did the judge have a
    change of heart?

'So the biggest thing happened.
The cop that died and got me locked up,
Frank Pheelan,
his wife told the judge she didn't wanna see me die.
She asked him to change the sentence.
Al's gonna make it part of the appeal
in Houston next week. What d'ya think?'

I think about how much
I need water.
I didn't drink enough today
while I worked on the car,

and the minestrone soup Sue made for lunch
was too salty.

'Does this stuff make a difference?' I ask.
And can Al even mention Pheelan's wife
at a state level appeal?
When Al explained the process he didn't tell me,
but I'm sure
Angela told me a long time ago
that they have rules about what can be raised
at each stage.

Ed's expression stiffens.
I've said something wrong.
'Sorry, I don't get the system. I don't ...' I tail off,
cos what I'm thinking is,

> *I don't know what to say to you, Ed,*
> *or how to say it.*
> *I shout at Angela*
> *cos I've known her my whole life.*
> *But I don't know what makes you tick*
> *or what would even happen if I shouted.*

Ed sniffs.
'I think it's *gotta* make a difference.

No way they can kill a man
when the victim's family says stop.
You know?'

I nod, eagerly this time.
'I see what you mean.'

Ed sits back in his chair. Sighs.
'Look, I know it's a long shot,
but Al says it can't hurt.'
He grins like a kid who's been
promised a chocolate dessert,
and it dawns on me that Ed
doesn't believe he's going to die;
he thinks Al will convince the judges
he never deserved any of this.

Water gurgles through a pipe on the wall.
I wipe my mouth with the back of my hand,
clear my throat.
It's hotter in here than out in the sun,
and that's saying something.

'You OK?' Ed asks.

'I'm thirsty is all,' I tell him.

He laughs. 'Oh, get used to that feeling, man.
You know they got air con in the main prison?
Air con and strawberry soap.
But you know what I'd love?
A Coke.'

I lower my gaze.
'I forgot to put money into your account,' I lie.

'Nah, that isn't what I meant.
Just gets to be a furnace in this place
and they don't go giving extras cos it's summer.
But I could destroy a cold Coke.
When it gets over a hundred,
I spend whole afternoons salivating
over soda cans and vending machines.
Like, you put your coins in,
the machine gobbles them – *clunk*, *clunk* –
and then – *bang* –
the can drops to the bottom
all cold and sweaty.
        Wet.
Thinking about that's like porn to me, man.'
He licks the air with his tongue.

I laugh loudly.

He laughs too,
and after a couple minutes we can't stop,
tears on our faces.

When the hour is up,
         I feel a whole lot better.

Ed's happy.
The cop's wife
could make a difference.

So maybe things will turn around.
I mean they could.

         It's not impossible.
         Not totally.

PHILIP MILLER

A fat guy in a tight shirt
smiles from behind an office window.
'Who's that?' I ask
as the guard retrieves my belongings from the locker.

She glances over her shoulder.
'That's Philip Miller, the warden.'

Mr Philip Miller,
father to a whole farm of lowlifes,
responsible for keeping them
chained down,
      locked up,
            sealed in,
so the rest of the state can sleep easy.

And he stands there
grinning.

The jackass.

THAT'S WHO

My face is in my phone,
distracting myself with Mets news,
      their win against Toronto.

But Ed is always there,
      in the corner of my mind,
      fidgeting.

What does he do to pass the time?
How can he stand it?
If that were me on the row,
I'd lie awake listening to killers snore,
imagining my walk to the death chamber,
      the length of the gurney,
      the smell and feel of the leather straps,
      the last faces I'd see –
the team doing the dirty work
and the guests in the gallery.

      What sort of asshole buys scratch cards
      instead of a soda for his dying brother?

Me,
that's who.

NIGHT RUN

I pull on my shorts and sprint full pelt
out of the building and
along Main Street,
past the gas station, motels,
pizza and fried chicken places,
until I reach the diner.

I couldn't run five thousand metres at this speed
but I'm not training.
I'm not running to strengthen my performance.
I even forgot to wear my watch.

I slow and peek through a side window to
see if Nell's at work.

She's not.

She's probably at home
watching TV or
eating ice cream.

Something normal,
        I guess.

Which is how I'd like my life to turn out.
Eventually.

TAILGATING

I slow my pace on my run home
when I come across a huddle of cars
belting out music in the high school parking lot.
Kids, kegs, buckets of chips.
I walk and watch.

A guy in a Houston Texans jersey
        guzzles a bottle of beer
then raises his head and roars at the sky
as though downing booze is a superpower.
He stumbles, trips,
                totally wasted.

I pass through the gates
and drift around until I spot two girls
by the trunk of a car
pouring vodka into a bowl.
'Hey,' I say.

The redhead looks up, eyes bloodshot.
'Hey,' she replies.

Her friend, a curly blonde,
whoops and wraps her arms around my neck.
She smells of aniseed.

'You came!' the blonde shouts, as though
expecting me.
'You're Lucy's cousin, right?
From Jacksonville?'
She dips a red cup into the bowl
        and offers it to me.
                It's sweet and toxic.

'I'm Peter,' I say,
so I don't have to answer her question.

They both do some sort of wormy dance,
hands twirling,
asses wriggling.
Behind them in the trunk is a phone,
a wallet.

'Lucy told us you were cool,' the redhead says.
'Where is Lucy anyway?'
She stands on tiptoe.

I take her hand,
twist her around so I've my back to the trunk
and she's looking at me, not for Lucy.

The blonde pours more sauce into my cup.
I knock it back in two seconds flat.

'Oh, you're a bad boy,' she whispers,
        lips brushing my ears.
But I'm not interested in being
a bad–boy–bit–of–rough,
a new guy who's
prime for picking
cos she thinks sex
is the most terrible thing she could ever do to her
lousy parents.

I wrap an arm around her waist,
put my other hand behind me,
find the wallet and
        slip it into the band of my shorts.
I thought it would be easy,
but I didn't think it would be this easy.

I'm about to give the girls some story about
locating Lucy
when someone taps my shoulder.

I turn.

It's Nell.
'Wanna take off?' she asks.

'Yes, please,' I say,
and follow her out of the parking lot
along the dusty, dark road
like a lost dog.

JUST NO

Nell leads me along the side entrance
to her yard.
She drops down into the deep end
of a dry-bottomed
swimming pool
and waves for me to follow.

'This is my dad's place.
Mom lives in Dover, next town over.'
She pulls a crushed joint from her pocket,
lights one end,
inhales like her life depends on it.

Night insects whinny to one another.
A car revs its engine, sounds its horn.
A dog is barking in the neighbour's yard.
'So, your *thing* is stealing stuff then?' she asks,
unimpressed.

I yank the wallet out of my shorts.
'I'll give the stuff back,' I say.
'I was looking for cash.'

Apart from some store loyalty cards
and a couple of photographs,
there's only ten bucks in it.
'I should have stolen her iPhone,' I say.

Nell snorts. 'In Wakeling?
You'd never sell it.
You'd get as far as *talking* about a stolen phone
and be down at the station.'
She grabs the wallet.
'I'll post it through Tanya's mailbox tomorrow.
Say I found it.'

'So you approve of theft?'

'I don't care what you do, Joe.'

'Are those girls your friends?'

'Friends? No. They'll be driving
rug rats around in minivans
before they're twenty years old.'

'You don't like minivans?'

She passes me the joint.
I inhale, hold it in my lungs,

let it run through my blood
until the tiles of the swimming pool
        soften against my back.

'No to minivans, little league and baking.
No to all that shit.
I'm not going to be a statistic.
I'm getting out of this hellhole alive
and I'll fight anyone who tries to stop me.
I want more.
But you can't say that too loudly round here
cos *who the hell do you think you are*, right?'

I exhale. 'I understand.'

She climbs the metal ladder
at the side of the swimming pool,
stands above me,
        a silhouette.
'I gotta go in.
And you better leave before my dad gets home.'

'Can I see you again?' I say aloud,
but under my breath mumble Nell's words:
        who the hell do you think you are?

SUPERHERO

Ed told me that when I got older
I could be anything I wanted.
'Can I be Spiderman?' I asked.
'Why not?' he said.
'And can I leave Arlington?'

He hesitated,
        just a second,
long enough for me to know something was up.

BEFORE THE SUN RISES

I wake at four thirty
and spend too long
calculating the number of days
left until Ed's execution.

It's July 9,
which gives us over a month
until August 18 –
not that Ed will see
any of his execution day;
he's scheduled to die a minute past midnight.

Ed will be cold
before the sun rises.

I peel myself out of bed and go for another run.

I want to improve my splits.

COUNTDOWN TO CHRISTMAS

As soon as Thanksgiving was done,
I wanted it to be Christmas,
daydreamed about all the toys
Santa Claus would place beneath the tree.
'He won't come if you're naughty,' Mom said,
scraping soggy cornflakes into the trash can.

Ed elbowed me,
    bit into a slice of burnt toast.
'Course he'll come, Joe.
You best write a letter
so you don't get a potato peeler.'

We wrote the letter together
and mailed it early,
asking for stuff I knew Mom couldn't afford,
that Santa's elves would make in the workshop –
a *Star Wars* Lego set,
a superhero costume,
a set of paints, glitter and bright white paper.
Could they sew together new sneakers?

While heavy snow fell
and the Hudson almost froze,

I counted off the days until Christmas.
And I never realised that the reason
Ed and Angela were so busy
shovelling sidewalks
was to make sure
I didn't cry with disappointment
on Christmas morning
and believe that Santa thought
I had been bad.

BREAKFAST BAGEL

Nell tosses me a plastic-wrapped bagel.
'Sue made it. Cream cheese and tomato.
And it's soup for lunch again, if you'll be here.'

'Thanks.'
        A dribble of sweat runs down my back.
'Hey, do you wanna hang out later?
We could get beers, sit in the back of the junker.'

Nell rubs the end of her nose.
'I don't think so,' she says.
Without an explanation,
        she returns to the diner.

I watch her go.

Has she searched Ed's name online?
Google would tell her everything she wanted to know
about him,
about me,
our whole family.

I bite into the bagel,
ticked off
Sue didn't send out a drink
to go with my breakfast.

FATHER MATTHEW

At the Section A entryway
an old guy with
soft eyes
approaches
        nervously.

Despite the heat
he's wearing a woollen sweater.
His beard has dandruff.

'I'm Father Matthew,
Ed's spiritual adviser.'
He holds out a hand and I shake it.
'And you're his brother Joseph?'

'Uh huh,' I mutter.

'I'm sorry you're going through this.'
He waves at the prison walls.

A grey-haired guard looks up from
her gossip magazine.

'I'm available for you too.
And anyone else in the family,' the priest continues.

'Look, Father …'

'Sometimes it's helpful to talk,' he says quickly.

I sniff.
Does he think I haven't talked about this already?
It's all Angela wants to discuss:
Ed's crime, case,
        how long he has left,
playing on a loop in her head.

'I'm here if you change your mind,' he says.
'Try to trust in God, son.'

Rage rushes through me
and I point
        my finger right between his eyes.
'You know what, Father?
God didn't put Ed in here.
Men did that.
And it's men keeping him here.
So go blow your God crap
at someone else, cos I'm not buying it.'

143

The priest doesn't flinch.
'Joseph –' he begins.

'My name's Joe,' I say.
'And you know nothing about me at all.'

PUBLIC RELATIONS

When the news broke in New York
that Ed was a suspected murderer,
kids in my class were warned by their petrified parents
to keep away from me,
the bad boy, sad boy,
God-only-knows-what-goes-on-behind-that-door boy.
Ed came from our house –
a place they suddenly assumed
was cooking up evil like
chicken soup.
It's not like they were the Gospel-spreading types;
half the neighbourhood were up to no good,
ducking taxes and stealing cable.

But Ed's crime put us in another league,
and that's where Aunt Karen stepped in –
she spat on us and shined us up to look
like a decent family,
stood in for Mom and Dad,
fed us and petted us,
        tried to turn things around.

And for this, I guess, I should be grateful.

But Karen never asked how happy we were or
what we wanted –
it was all about how things looked from
          the outside;
what other people thought
was all that was important,
and how we felt about ourselves was irrelevant.
Our desires didn't matter.

Karen stole Ed from us
and
we'll never get those years back.

THE WALL

Ed's knuckles are bruised a plummy purple.
He rubs them and laughs.
'You think *this* is something?
In here? Joe, this is nothing.'

'Why'd you fight?'
I want to hear how he defended himself
against the toughest guys,
lunatics locked up for burying people alive,
monsters who are nothing like him.

'They wouldn't let me shower,' he says.
'I missed my slot, so now I stink.'

'Who'd you hit?'

He looks ashamed.
            Was it Father Matthew?
            A guard?
'I punched a wall,' he says.
'And I know this looks painful,
but you should see the wall.'

He winks
and the rest of the visit goes great.

A JOKE

Al Mitchell meets me by the prison gates
and shakes my hand like I'm a man.
'Good to meet you, Joe.
Let's take a walk,' he says,
but we don't go far
before he stops
and kicks a stone
with the toe of his leather loafer.
'I was in Houston today.
The state denied our appeal. I'm sorry.
The cop's wife wants the sentence commuted to life
but she's not the one prosecuting Ed –
the state's doing that.
Anyway, the judge wasn't interested in her letter.
Listened with one ear, you know?
The Supreme Court will be more impartial.
If we can get the federal court to hear us,
we have a real chance of winning.
This isn't over.'

'What can I do?'

He rests a hot hand on my arm.
'Keep your fingers crossed.'

Is that it?
Is this all down to luck?
The judge Ed gets, the jury?
'Justice is a joke,' I say.

Al nods.
'Look, Joe, this process will change you.
I've seen it plenty of times.
I've felt it myself in my heart.
What's happening is hell,
and as long as you survive,
you've done well.'
He squeezes my arm and I don't pull away,
don't play the tough guy to fend him off.

Instead I ask,
'What are his chances?'

Al's cell phone rings.
Without glancing at it, he clicks it off –
shuts out whoever needs him.
It's a little thing, ignoring that call,
but it means a lot.

'We still have options,' he says vaguely,
and turning us around,

heads back to death row
so he can break the bad news
to my brother.

MY LIFE NOW

I run to Nell's place quickly –
my splits around ten seconds quicker than usual.
I want to hang out with her,
chill in her backyard and guzzle beer.
Or we could sip water.
Whatever.
Anything.

But there's a blue truck in the driveway.
        The same truck that picked her up
        from the gas station.

So I return to the apartment,
put a frozen pizza in the oven
and set an alarm to beep after twelve minutes.

Angela calls and we talk about
the weather – compare New York summers
to Texan ones.

This is my life now.

THE PROSECUTOR

The morning news features Ed's story again –
his mean mugshot,
his handsome victim,
the state attorney
outside the courthouse
yesterday
looking so pleased with himself
you'd think he'd won
first prize in a meat raffle.

The state attorney puffs up his chest,
presses his mouth to the microphones.
'We are delighted that
Judge Byron did not reverse the decision
made by the original trial judge and jury,
nor saw any valid reason for a retrial.'

Cameras flash,
        questions are asked
and the prosecutor beams,
dying to elaborate
and spout hate against Ed.

I turn the TV off;
I hate his face.

THE COST

It costs around four million dollars
to go through with an execution.
That's eight times more money
than to imprison someone for life.
Not that anyone gives a damn:
killing is worth every cent.

WHERE IT ENDS

Ed talks like a high-speed train.
'I seen over a hundred guys in this place
      go to the chamber,
and every one thought he'd get off in the end.'
He scratches his head.
'And you know what's really screwed up?
When those guys said goodbye
they didn't do it properly cos
they thought that a minute before midnight
the governor would *ring-a-ding-ding*
and say they've made a massive mistake.
But this isn't the movies.
No one's walking out the front door in a suit.
When folks here say you're for the gurney,
they aren't messing around.
The only way out is in a box.'
He laughs bitterly.

I don't know this Ed.
So far I've only seen
the one who believes it'll be OK.

'This is where it ends, Joe,' he whispers.
'I'm telling you the truth.'

MY VERSION

He leans on a row of railings,
chews on gum
and pretty confidently squints away the sun.
He's older than me,
    but not by much.

'Joe?' he wants to know.
He's too friendly.

'Have we met?'

He picks up a canvas satchel,
throws it across his body,
runs and stumbles to get to me
before I'm through the prison gates.
His shirtsleeves are rolled up,
shoes scuffed.

'How did Ed cope with losing his appeal?' he asks.
He lets his head fall to one side in sympathy
and I know then who he is and what he wants –
even Karen's takeover at home all those years ago
couldn't keep the newshounds from the door.

'I'm not talking to the press,' I hiss.

He holds up his hands.
'Dude, I just wanna know how Ed's holding up.
Maybe you guys want *your* story told.
Your version of things.'

'My *story*? This isn't a story,
        you asshole.
This is my life.'
I make my expression mean.
'You interested in knowing more about me?
You wanna see the kind of guy I can be?'

He comes closer
        so we're chin-to-chin.
'You know what, dude,
that would also make an excellent story.'
He laughs, taunting me,
steps back and with his phone snaps a photo.

'What's going on?'
a guard calls out,
inspecting us from Section A,
a hand on his holster.

My anger bubbles.

But it won't do Ed any good getting into a fight.

'My brother's innocent,' I snarl.

'Write *that* in your stupid paper.'

INNOCENT

Is Ed innocent?
I mean,
I've never actually asked him outright.

THE TIP JAR

Sue's lips are pinched around the
      butt of her cigarette.
'Any luck with the car today, hun?' she asks.

'Nah. But I'll try again tomorrow.'
I take a seat at the counter
where Sue ladles lentils
from a copper pot into a brown bowl,
plops it in front of me.
'I've plenty, so shout if you're still hungry.'

I slurp at the soup,
glance up at the wall clock.
Fifty minutes until visiting time.
'Hey, Sue,
I don't suppose you could spare a few bucks
so I can catch a bus?
I'll give it back.'
I hate myself for asking
but I'm tired of trekking through the humidity.

Sue slides her tip jar,
filled with
crumpled dollar bills

and multicoloured coins,
across the counter.
'Ain't much, but take what you need.'

'I'll pay it back. I promise.'

Sue pats my hand.
'Relax and eat your lunch, hun.'

BAD NEWS

The diner door pings and Nell appears.
She doesn't see me at first,
hums her way to the counter
swinging a set of car keys.
'Thanks for taking such a late lunch order,'
she tells Sue.
'Daddy's at home
and all we have in the house is cheese string.'

'Gimme a sec.'
Sue disappears into the kitchen.

Nell sits on a stool next to me.

'You're avoiding me,' I say.
'Like, just a fraction?'

She reaches for a menu to fan her face.
'Shit. I thought I was being subtle about it.'

'Not really.
I mean,
one night we're hanging out, then I never see you.
I feel used.'

I keep my voice light
so she thinks I'm teasing.

But Nell is serious.
'Look, Joe, I'm bad news to you.'

I force a laugh.
'I love bad news.'

Then Sue is beside us with a bag.
She shifts from one foot
        to the other.
'Here's your order, hun.'

Nell sighs.
'Thanks, Sue.'
She turns to me.
'Look, I've no interest in making fast friends.'

'Me neither,' I tell her.
And I mean it.
'I'm in Texas for Ed.'

'See you around,' she says.
        And she's gone.

A SODA

'I got a soda
with the money you put into the account,' Ed says.

'I didn't send it,' I admit,
wondering if Angela managed to find funds
after I told her Karen had been sending Ed money
every month
but had stopped.

'Well, whatever, man.
God, it was sweet. Best soda ever.'
His eyes well up
and I want to reach through the Plexiglas,
grab him, shake him,
tell him to get a grip;
            it's just a soda.

Jesus, Ed, it's just a fucking soda.

But it isn't.
It isn't just a soda at all.

PEOPLE HERE

I'm on Main Street minding my own business
when a woman
      with a poodle under one arm
      murmurs something.

'Excuse me?'

'Your brother killed a police officer,' she says
and shakes a newspaper at me,
noses the air.

So the journalist published a piece and pointed to me.
And here we go again – guilt by association,
strangers scared of my dangerous DNA.

'He isn't guilty,' I tell her.
I seem to be saying this a lot
when I've no idea how true it is.

'People around here hope he fries,' she spits,
just like that,
      straight into my face.

I take a deep breath.

'They don't use the chair any more.

So no one's getting fried. Sorry.'

    I pat the poodle

    and continue along the street.

WITHOUT THE CONS

Sue brews me tea and
pushes a large jelly doughnut
  across the counter.
'That old witch don't talk for the rest of us, Joe.
Wakeling wouldn't last a day without the cons.
Whole damn town is financed by the farm.'

I bite into the doughnut. It's still warm.
'Can I have a tenderloin
with peppercorn sauce for lunch?' I ask.

Sue laughs.
'You can have a substandard burger and cold fries.'

'Is that all you think I'm worth?'
I'm trying to make Sue smile
but she scrutinises me.

'Real question is what you think
you're worth, hun.'

DAD

It's not like they *all* ran away.
Dad was different.
I've seen pictures of him rocking me
with cheaply tattooed arms,
face furrowed from years of unemployment lines
and dealing crystal meth to junkies
who'd have cut him
rather than let him leave
without their hit.

But he died before I was a year old,
got himself killed:

                 billiard ball hidden in a sock
                 to the back of the head,
                 like a real hero.

And the guy who did it?
Claimed it was an accident,
served four and a half years on Rikers Island,
      which seems,
      I don't know,
a fucking disgrace
after everything that's happened to Ed.

NELL SENDS A MESSAGE

Come over to my house later.

I don't know how she got my number,
probably from Sue,
but it doesn't matter.
      She wants to see me.

ASK HIM

We are in Nell's swimming pool again.
She scatters shreds of weed on top of the tobacco.
'You look like a hillbilly hen farmer.
Wear some sunscreen.'

My arms are peeling red.
My face must be worse.
'Back in New York this isn't who I am,' I say.
'I got a kind of a life.'

She lights the tip of the roll-up and inhales,
          passes the joint.
'Sue said your brother killed a cop.
I looked him up.
He was young when it happened.
Like, our age.'

I breathe in the bud, cough,
and she smacks my back.
She takes the joint from me,
pinches the butt between her fingers,
doesn't put the paper to her mouth.
'Did he do it?'

'No!'
My voice is sharper, louder than I intend.

She hesitates.
'But he's still got appeals and stuff, right?
I mean ...'

'He's got the Supreme Court,
if they agree to hear the case.
And the governor as a very last resort.'

'So what happened?
Why'd they lock him up?'

'He confessed to it,' I tell her.

'But if he didn't do it,
            why'd he say he *did*?'

'I dunno.'
And I've never
            asked Ed outright,
not even since I started visiting.
Why is that?
            What is it about Ed's story
            that makes me doubt him?

Nell reads my mind.
'I'd wanna know exactly what happened
so I could get it neat in my head.'

She's right.
I need the truth,
whatever shape it comes in.
I need to know Ed trusts me,
that we have no secrets between us,
no bullshit
now we're so close to the end.
We were always good friends.
I want him to tell me everything.

'Ask him,' Nell says.

ED CONFESSED TO THE CRIME

Back when it happened,
Ed signed a sworn statement confessing
to shooting Frank Pheelan.

He told Mom on the phone
the cops forced him to sign
and he was too tired and confused to argue.

Little else links him to the crime.

This is all I know.

POINTLESS

The walls are sweating.
It must be a hundred and ten degrees
in the visiting room.
'I'm learning Spanish,' Ed says, in greeting.

'Huh?'

'Spanish.
I figure I'm from New York
and I've been in Texas
for ten years so
there's no excuse.
Half the guys here speak it,
but to get good you gotta study.
Anyway, now I got Al
I can give up the law stuff.
Gotta fill my time somehow, right?'

I'm not sure what to say,
but I'm careful not to blurt out,
What's the point?

Ed counts to ten in Spanish,
tells me his name and where he lives.

I listen and eventually Ed simmers down.
'Do you speak another language?'
He wipes his forehead with the back of his hand.

My throat is chalk dry.
I shake my head. 'I hardly speak English.'

He laughs and there is a lull,
                  a conspicuous
                    gap in the conversation,
a space for a question.

'Ed, I have something to ask.'

He pulls his chair closer,
like that makes a difference.
'I'm right here, man.'
His eyes are wide, waiting to give me advice,
        be a big brother.

It's always so damn hot here.
And they never set out water
or put a fan in the room.

'Joe?' Ed looks concerned.

I mean, the irony of it –
he looks concerned for *me*.

'I gotta ask …' I try.
But I can't.
I stare at him.
And he stares right back.

For a long time.

Time:
      the very thing we don't have to waste.

DID YOU DO IT?

'Did you kill that cop?'

WRONG

Ed removes the receiver from his ear and
squints at it like something might be
wrong with the prison equipment.

AGAIN

'What happened back then?'
            My voice is tinny.
I should shut up and let Ed answer,
but quickly new questions come and
            I spit them at him.
'Why did you confess?
Why didn't the old lawyer do the talking?
Wasn't there DNA to prove you never did it?'

Ed taps the table with his fingertips.
'You really gonna ask me that?'

I grit my teeth.
'I have to know one hundred per cent, Ed.'

'You're *really* asking me this stuff?'
He drops the phone.
The sound splinters my eardrum.

Then he stands and
            before I can do anything about it
is shackled and shuffling away.

'Ed. Talk to me!' I shout.
'Why can't we just talk about it?'

But it's too late.

He's gone.

Again.

IN ME

Before Ed got arrested,
Angela never stopped believing
he would come back
of his own accord
once he quit being mad with Mom.

I knew better.
Ed was stubborn.

I knew better.
I had more Ed in me than
I've ever admitted.

THE WARDEN

What I definitely do not need
as I leave
is Philip Miller waiting for me.

'You got two seconds, son?'
I don't know where he gets off
          flashing that big, bogus smile
when he's the one who'll
put Ed down in the end.

In his office
we face one another,
a bulky desk between us
piled high with books
and paper cups.

'We haven't spoken.
My name's Philip Miller,
though I figure you already know that.'
He pauses,
like maybe I'm meant to
acknowledge his power.

I clench my jaw,
turn my hands into fists.

On his desk is a photograph of a girl in roller skates,
yellow dungarees,
her hair held up in lopsided bunches.

'It can't be easy,' he says.

'No,' I admit,
'but at least I'm not organising the injection.'

He straightens his tie,
dabs his clammy forehead with a Kleenex.
'I'm doing my job, Joseph,' he says,
like that's an excuse,
like that isn't what the prosecutor says,
the judge, the jury, the guards.

'I guess the Nazis claimed the same thing,' I say.
I don't know a lot about history,
but I do understand that all it takes
is a whole bunch of bystanders
and people just doing their jobs
for ugly things to happen.

His smile fades.
'I wanted to introduce myself and reassure
you that my staff will be respectful
throughout this process.

I understand *you* committed no crime, after all.
Is there anything the prison can help with?'
He's trying to be considerate,
smooth over his guilt with bullshit benefits.

'You got a crucifix on the wall,' I say.

He nods;
        he knows what's coming
        and doesn't try to stop me.

'I wonder what Jesus would do
if he were here for a day.'

Philip Miller stands.
The meeting is over.
'Come see me if you need anything,' he says.

BRAVE NEW WORLD

Nell is perched on the kerb
near the gas station,
a book balanced on her knees.
Her plimsolls rest on a beaten-up skateboard
covered in oversized stickers.
'You been waiting long?' I ask.

She holds up her book: *Brave New World*.
'I've read fifty-four pages of this tripe,
so yeah, pretty much been here a lifetime.'
She stands and dusts herself off.
'Wanna go for a lemonade?'

'A what?'
The last thing I want is a soft drink.
I need to get numb.

'Lemonade, Joe.
It's a drink for quenching a thing called thirst.'
She punches me full force in the thigh,
folds over the book and stuffs it into the
back pocket of her shorts.
'Come on.'

A DECENT MAN

A fancy street,
lawns decorated in rockeries
and a small stand where giddy girls
sell homemade lemonade
for fifty cents a pop.

Nell pays with a balled-up dollar bill
and we sit on the wall outside the girls' house.

'Did you see him?' she asks.

I sip, slurp, gulp.
'I've screwed everything up.'

    She puts a hand on my arm.
    I fix my eyes on her fingers,
    the broken, unpolished nails.

'But it got me thinking,' I go on.
'Why wouldn't he answer?'

She sighs
like she might understand,

but she can't know how much I need Ed
to tell me he didn't do it – could *never* do it –
that evil isn't threaded through our genes
like everyone thinks.

What I need is for Ed to say
that I have a fighting chance
of becoming a decent man
someday.

ED WON'T SEE ME

So I trudge back to town
in the pot-roast heat
and work on the junker.

AND THE NEXT DAY

It is the same.

NOT DRIVING

Nell and I share a booth and drink Oreo milkshakes.
She's almost finished *Brave New World*,
turns the pages so violently
she's in danger of ripping them.
'Quit reading it,' I tell her.

'I want to have an opinion,' she says.

'What? I got opinions on a ton of stuff
I know nothing about.
Like ... oysters.'

'Oysters?'

'Yeah – I've never eaten one but they're gross.
And surfing. It's stupid. Arrogant.
Also, New Jersey.
Armpit of the universe.
I mean, who'd live in Hoboken?'

She thumps my leg.
'You're a genuine jackass.'

'I know,' I say,
and look out the window.

Her fingers tap my arm.
'I'm sure he'll see you tomorrow,' she says.

THE THIRD DAY

'He has to see me,' I say.

The marine–guard is back.
He shrugs and
makes a *not-much-I-can-do* face.

'Fine. Pass on a message.
Tell Ed from me that he's a prick.'

HALLOWEEN

I was a werewolf
howling into the October sky,
fake fur fastened to my face.
Angela took me trick-or-treating
and we filled two buckets with candy.
At home, Ed laughed at my costume:
'Are you meant to be a scary beaver?'
I got so irate I stormed down to our room
and refused to come out.
Ed said it was a joke,
wouldn't apologise.
And even though we both
sulked for a few days,
by the end of it we were
friends
and couldn't
remember why it had got us all
steamed up in the first place.

CHARITY

A thin tap on my apartment door.
'From Ed,' Father Matthew says,
holding out an envelope.
He peers into the gloom behind me.

'I'd invite you in
but I don't own a coffee pot
and the water runs yellow,' I explain.

He waves away the suggestion.
'Maybe I can get you a drink in town?'

Some company would be nice,
but there's a limit to how much charity I can take.
I've reached it.
'I don't think so.'

'Another time maybe,' he says. 'Goodnight, Joe.'

'Goodnight, Father.'

ANOTHER LETTER

Dear Joe,

So here it is:

      I was driving real late on Route 35
      just north of New Braunfels.
      That's true what they said,
            I was there that night
            and I got pulled over.
      The cop was mad as hell before I even spoke.
      He checked my licence but I didn't have
      registration documents for the wheels
      cos they was Aunt Karen's –
      I never lied about that.
      He said he had to call it in.
      I panicked, man.
      I thought he'd see the car was Karen's
      and take me to the station.
      I didn't wanna go back to Staten Island.
      I didn't wanna live with Mom.
      So when he got on his radio, I split.
      I know it was stupid but I wasn't
      thinking straight.

Anyway,

      I caught the cop by surprise
      and he had to run his ass back to the cruiser.

But I had my foot to the floor and was gone.
Didn't even see him in the rear-view cos
I came off the highway quick as I could,
      took some back roads.

Thing is,

I was low on gas so I pulled into a
Taco Bell. I remember that cos I was dead hungry.
I ditched the car there and took off,
walked to a bus station.
I seen heaps of people along the road
and no one took any notice of me.
I was real glad they didn't that day,
but after I wished I'd looked hard in
someone's eye
so they could tell the jury they'd seen me,
you know, seen me and I wasn't
covered in blood.

Anyway,

I took a bus south, the hell out of Comal County.
And I was sitting on that bus busting my ass laughing
cos I thought I got away with it.
I imagined Karen would get her car back
but I'd still be missing, which is what I wanted.
Easy, right?

So,

the next week I'm pumping gas for tips in
San Antonio,
not thinking about that cop stopping me.
I mean, he got my licence but it's the
Staten Island address.
Then I get picked up.
Just like that.
These rookie cops pull into the station for air
and take me in.
I told them again and again
how it happened,
that I got stopped and got scared and bolted.
But they started talking about a gun
and that's when I got real confused,
told them I didn't even own a gun.

Anyway,

I go into the station at midnight and they leave me
in an interrogation room for hours,
though there's no record of that.
Then they say they got a lawyer coming
and was I OK answering some questions
before the lawyer got there cos it was late?

Well,

they tricked me right, cos no public defender's
coming to a station at three in the morning,

196

but I said – sure I can answer your questions –
cos I didn't do anything, so I wasn't too worried,
figured Karen would be pissed about her wheels
but wouldn't press charges.
I know they have zilch on me.
But they get mean, telling me I'm white trash.
And they give me a lie detector test and start
asking crazy questions about a cop
and a shooting and a murder
and I got no idea at all what's happening.

Anyway,

later I heard I passed that damn test,
but they tell me I failed.

Now,

it's 8 o'clock in the morning and I've no lawyer.
They say I'm lying, the test doesn't make mistakes.
They show me some papers,
like I can understand them.
They say maybe I shot a cop by accident cos
I was scared
and I say no – that's not what happened –
the cop was alive when I drove away.
They say judges go easy on cons who confess,
that if I lie they'll give me the death penalty
and do I know how it feels to get
put to sleep like a bitch?

I ask for my lawyer and they say he's coming.
I ask could I get some water and they say sure
                    but they never bring it.
I ask can I sleep cos by then it was the afternoon
and I thought I was gonna fall over.
So one officer says yeah, I can sleep.
But he doesn't take me back to the cell.
He takes me to a cruiser with some other cop
and they drive me to a street with no lamps,
make me get out of the car.

So,

I can't see any people or houses or anything.
Just sort of a swamp. And the cops
put a gun to my head
and say they know I'm a killer
and I'm gonna confess cos if I don't
they'll make sure I get what's coming.
And you know, I was thinking
that if I had skills and could get that gun,
I'd shoot him for trying to spook me.

So,

what would you have done, Joe?
I figured I didn't have a choice,
so I go back to the station and tell them everything
I think I heard them tell me about
what happened to the cop.

I said it, then signed a paper just before
my lawyer shows up and shakes his head
and asks why I did it

cos

he knows
that it doesn't matter whether you're innocent or not –
if they have a confession, a jury is gonna believe it.

But

I was only eighteen and I was thinking
I could sign and later tell people what happened
                    by that road
and they'd believe me cos why would someone confess
then change his mind?

But that signature did me in.

Judge let them use it in court even though
I didn't have a lawyer when I signed
and the confession had no details about the murder,
nothing that proves I knew what happened.

You know,

when I was giving that confession,
I asked for Mom.
That's sort of stupid I know,
but I was crying and I wanted Mom to get me out.

But we both know
she couldn't get herself out of a paper bag
if it was on fire.
Thing was,
I didn't understand that
the cop who stopped me the week before was dead.
Shot.
Routine stop a couple hours after mine.
Camera in the cop car wasn't working,
but the last call he made was when he busted me
and they had my picture, so every crooked cop
in the state was looking for me –
I was a celeb in Texas and didn't even know it.
Face was even on the news.
So,
they got me and they had to get someone
cos a cop was dead and what they gonna do.
Let a cop case go unsolved?
People care big time about white police officers
and I'm just surprised they never tried to
stitch up some black guy. Loads of black guys
on the row say they got stitched up
and you gotta believe them
if you see the news and all these cops
shooting guys cos they're
walking down a dark street or whatever.

So,

> *it took the jury an hour to find me guilty.*
> *An hour, man.*
> *I waited for trains longer than that.*
> *Never good when a jury comes back quick —*
> *that's what they say.*

There it is, Joe.

> *Black and white.*
> *Is this the stuff you wanted to know*
> *straight from my mouth?*

Joe,

> *I'd believe a confession if I didn't know*
> *how the damn things come about.*
> *I'd think,*
> *why would you admit to something you didn't do?*

But still,

> *I'm sore as hell.*
> *Cos you gonna ask me now?*
> *This late in the game?*
> *I got guys who never asked me.*
> *Like Tyler in the cell next to mine — he knows the truth.*

Thing is,

> *he admitted what he did — killed his girl.*
> *Took a week for the cops to find her,*
> *and you know what?*

I could tell him if I was guilty and
he wouldn't bat an eyelash
cos what he did was so dirty.
But he knows I'm not made like him.

Thing is,

if you lie about murder on the row
it makes you the worst sort of scum.
That's why guys end up telling more than their share.

Like last year,

Colin McConnors admitted
doing in those hitchhikers in Alaska,
though no one even knew he was in Fairbanks
when it happened.
We wasn't surprised cos McConnors is a sicko.
The crime they got him for was rotten.

Weird thing is,

McConnors is OK when you talk one to one.
He likes chess and politics.
He's got smarts too.
Reads all sorts of books by Russians
and spouts Shakespeare like a boss.

So,

you asked me to tell the truth,
kind of saying I didn't already,
so maybe I was a real scumbag,

worse than McConnors, someone who's
gonna lie
to save my own ass.
Well, that isn't me.
Anyway,
    I'm not writing to tell you to go screw it.
    I missed you and I thought about you every day
    for ten years,
    I swear.
    Come visit me again.
    I've not got long and I don't wanna waste any
    more time
    being vexed.
    And you gotta stop
    wasting time wondering
    whether or not
    I'm lying.
    And maybe you gotta stop being vexed too,
    cos I seen some rage in you,
    quietly burbling, man.
    See you tomorrow, yeah?
    Ed x

NO LIES

There are no lies in Ed's eyes.
Just hurt.
'I don't know where to start,' I say.

'The letter made sense?' he asks.

'Yes,' I say.
The letter told me he was framed,
so that's what I'm going to believe.

'You need me to tell it to your face?' he asks.
His voice is barbed.

'Of course not,' I say,
then realise I *do* need that,
no matter the outcome.
'Maybe,' I admit.

Ed shakes his head.
'I'm trying not to be hurt, man.
But it's hard when your own blood won't believe you.
No one will listen.
I wanted one person on my side, and that was you.'

He cracks his knuckles against the desk,
gestures for me to get closer to the glass.
'I didn't kill Frank Pheelan.
I never touched a hair on his head.
I was a petty thief when I came down to Texas,
but I've never been a murderer.'
He clenches his jaw.

'I had to ask. I *had* to,' I say.

He shrugs. 'OK.'

'I also have to tell you something.'

He narrows his eyes impatiently.
'What is it?'

'I'd still be sitting here if you did it.
I'd know you didn't deserve *this*.'

      He blinks.
      I clench my fists.

'No one does, man,' he says.
'And I can say that cos I live it.
Anyone who disagrees oughta try it out for a day.'

He pauses.
'What does it matter?
No one cares.
You know they got petitions
to stop us getting medical care cos of the cost?'

'Who does?'

'Crazy people,' he says, and laughs.
'*Way* crazier than any of us.
And the worst thing is,
they're on the outside walking free.'

RESPONSIBLE

They charged Ed as an adult,
locked him up and
sentenced him to die
three years before
anyone thought
he was old enough
to buy a beer in a bar.

WITH NELL

Nell drops down
into the swimming pool then
     shunts away
so we aren't touching.

'He didn't do it,' I tell her.
'He was a dropout, but not a killer.
I don't know why I had to ask.
I knew him back then.'

I study her face under the dim moon,
wishing she'd move closer,
wishing I could be less of a creep
and just enjoy what we have –
stop wanting more.

Then she takes my hand.
It's sweaty, but so is mine.
'Wanna watch *Armageddon*?
Bruce is, like, an awesomely hot dad in it.'

'That would be cool,' I say,
     and we go inside.

WE DON'T KISS

We don't even keep holding hands.
We watch *Armageddon* and
eat marshmallows.
That's all.

It's a pretty great night.

THE CEILING FAN

The ceiling fan doesn't spin,
won't turn and churn
any sort of air around the room.
I glare at it from the bed
and then,
without really wanting to,
think of Nell.
Is she showering?
Sleeping?
Between sheets smelling soapy?

I want these thoughts to stir me, but they don't.
All I feel is loss,
an ache nowhere near my pants
but up in my chest
        and in my arms too.
I want to hold on to her,
have her lie on me – feel her full weight
pinning me down.

And I want to message her,
say goodnight,
but don't want to chase her away.
I plug in my phone on the other side of the room
so I can't check it every seven seconds.

I turn over,
      imagine Nell is next to me.
It makes me smile. It makes me sad.

I squeeze my eyes shut.
I wish the damn ceiling fan would work.

ROUTINE

Every morning
I work on the junker in the sun
and it never turns over.
Every afternoon
I visit Ed and we pretend that talking
through glass is normal.
Every afternoon
Angela calls to tell me she's working hard for tips,
that she'll
be in Wakeling soon.
Every night
Nell and I hang out –
    and it helps the other stuff
    seem a bit less
    crappy.

ANGELA CALLS

'Hey … Ange …' I pant,
putting my mouth under the kitchen faucet,
gulping in lukewarm water
after my run.
'You find a flight?'

She clicks her tongue.
'I'm gonna call Aunt Karen and ask for a loan.
How you doing for cash?' she asks.

'Don't worry about me.
And don't ask Karen.
If she doesn't care, she doesn't care.'

Angela is mute. Guilty.
But none of this is her fault.
We're doing our best,
and if *I* was the one with the job
then she'd be down here with Ed
instead of me.

Maybe I should blame Aunt Karen.
Or I could get pissed at Mom, Dad,
the State of Texas.

I could make a list, rank the culprits:
> *And making a new entry this week*
> *at No.5 is Ed's arresting officer ...*

'Joe?' Angela whispers.

'I'm here,' I tell her.

'I know,' she says.
'And I'm coming soon.'

USA

Another press conference was held in Houston
last night,
          aired on breakfast news.
It was following a Republican Party fundraiser.
Governor McDowell had eaten a five course meal
followed by Scotch and cigars.
He'd met Miss USA
in her winning pink sash
and they'd posed for photos.

And McDowell, nicely juiced, stood at a podium
and said it was 'premature'
to offer Ed executive clemency
and he'd be 'waiting for the court's decision'
before reviewing the case again.

Then he climbed into a chauffeur–driven Cadillac.
I'm guessing he slept pretty soundly
in a Hilton penthouse suite.
I'm guessing he didn't dream of needles but
maybe he did think about
Miss USA and her pretty pink sash.

Ed's life is in this guy's hands.

IF

Al Mitchell calls.
'Try not to worry.
These things often go down to the wire.'

'But if the Supreme Court refuse to hear Ed's case
or deny his appeal,
that asshole will be the only person
with any power to postpone the execution.
It isn't right.'
I am ranting.
I can hear myself.

Al sighs.
I can't tell whether he's frustrated with me
or annoyed with McDowell.
        Maybe it's neither of those things.
        He has his own life after all.
'It's bullshit. I agree.
And your brother's case is based on a false confession.
If I'd been the defence lawyer back then …'
He sighs again.

'You're his lawyer now,' I say,
trying to bolster the guy
who's meant to be bolstering me.

'Yeah,' he says,
'And I promise.
I'm doing everything I can.'

THIRTY MINUTES

Ed's eyes are bloodshot,
cheeks a little sunken.
'I've not been sleeping,' he says.
He rubs his face with both hands.
'I heard from Mom.'
He smirks
      and I wonder if it's a joke.

'You what?'

'Our beloved mother called.
Warden let me talk to her for thirty minutes.'

'Thirty minutes?'
It's been years since I've spoken to Mom.
I don't even know what her voice sounds like.

'She wanted to know how I was.
Wanted to know about this place,
how the guards treat us.
She asked how long she's got to come visit.
I swear, man,
      she said it like I was moving house.'

He turns to the pale guard
     standing behind him,
         grins like we're all sharing a joke.

'Mom's gonna visit?' I ask.
My heart beats hard.

He sneers. 'What do *you* think?
I told her we'd get it figured out.
She cried,' he says.
'Real blubber show.
But those tears weren't for me, man –
she just wanted to be forgiven.'
He pauses.
'She asked about you and Angela.'

I am silent.

'And you know what?'
     He leans forward.
'I could hear a TV.
She never even turned off the TV to call me.'
He laughs.
'What do you think of that?'

AUNT KAREN CALLS

'Joe? It's me.'
Her voice is as hard
as the stone in an apricot.
'Hi, Aunt Karen.'
'Are you still in Wakeling?'
'Yeah.'
'And you're alive?'
'I am.'
'And Ed's coping?'
'I guess,' I say.
'Well, that's fine then,' she replies,
and without
    any goodbye
    closes the phone.

My first thought:
    I didn't hear the sound of any TV
    in the background.

STRICT

For my eleventh birthday I wanted to go to a
football game.
'I haven't money for that,' Aunt Karen complained.
So instead she made a chocolate cake,
used M&Ms to write my name,
KitKat sticks for the frame.
She stuck eleven red candles in it, lit them and
we sang 'Happy Birthday'
before eating our spaghetti bolognese,
the cake for dessert only.
Dad was gone ten years.
Ed was gone four.
Mom had left the previous summer.

Aunt Karen was under no obligation to stay.
'It's like being in the military,' Angela and I said,
wishing she'd disappear and leave us to
have parties and eat junk food.
      But at least there was milk in the fridge
      and clean clothes in the closets.
Usually we were glad Aunt Karen was
      tougher than
      anyone else.
Usually we were glad she hadn't bailed.

THE WORST THING

'What's the worst thing you've ever done?' I ask Nell.

She bites into the steak sandwich
Sue sent out for me,
           then hands it over.
'Needs more onion,' she says.

'So? The worst thing?' I repeat.

'Yeah, chill out, I'm thinking.'
She examines the engine with her fingertips.
'I yelled at my dad,' she says.

She fiddles with the oil cap,
and I can't tell if she's being sarcastic.
'I told him he was going to hell.'

'Why?'

'Cos of what he's responsible for.'
She isn't looking at me.
Her fingertips are greasy now.

'Does he hurt you?'

She sniffs.
'No,' she says. 'He loves me.
That's the thing.
He's this big, gentle guy.
But he …
We're always arguing.
It's my fault.
He's nice to me.
I just can't be kind back.'

'Why not?'

She looks away.
'Doesn't matter.
        Anyway, what about you?'

I've made out with my friends' girlfriends,
stolen stuff,
beaten up guys for no good reason.
I hated Mom for leaving and hoped she'd die,
hated Karen for caring and hoped she'd leave.

'I rarely admit I have a brother,' I tell her.
'When I meet new people,
I pretend Ed doesn't exist
so I won't have to explain.

And now it's looking like he might not exist.
So yeah.
That's the worst thing.'

Nell wipes her hands on her shirt.
'You didn't make this happen,' she says.
'And you know what else?'
         She steps towards me,
              touches my elbow.
'We aren't the worst things we did
or the worst things that happened to us.
We're other stuff too.
Like …
We're the times we made cereal
or watched *Buffy the Vampire Slayer*
or helped an old lady off a bus.
We're the good, the bad, and the stupid, right?'
She smiles and
grabs the steak sandwich like it
spoke out of turn.
'I'll eat this and get you something else.
What do you want?'

Should I say, *I want you, Nell*?

'You stay there and mull it over.
I'll get you a cheeseburger.'

'Actually the steak sandwich looked good.'

'Well, it's too late. Last of the meat.'
She bites into it again.
'But it definitely needs more onion.
Like, *loads* more.'

POSSIBLE

Before I take off,
Sue comes out.
She peers under the hood.
'Maybe you should find another job.'

'You fed up feeding me?' I ask.

She pokes me in the arm.
'It's breaking my heart
    watching you melting out here,' she says.
'Lenny told me it's hopeless.'

'Not hopeless,' I say. 'Just difficult.'

'*Really* difficult,' she says.

'But possible,' I remind her.
'I mean, anything's possible.'

TOM HANKS

Ed isn't wearing the usual shackles
around wrists and ankles.
And the warden is with him,
        behind him.
He pats Ed's back as
my brother sits.
Philip Miller mutters something before
wandering away.

Ed picks up the phone.
'Jesus, Joe, you been grilled like bacon!'
He laughs.
His guard can't help grinning either.

I touch my forehead,
beet red and peeling.
It kind of hurts too.
'What did the warden want?' I ask.

'Ah, he's just saying thanks for getting
Tom Hanks to take a shower.'

Is Ed going nuts?
It happens to guys on death row,

which wouldn't be such a bad thing.
I mean,
          you can't execute a lunatic.
'Tom Hanks?' I ask.

'That's what we started calling Kierney.
You seen *Cast Away*?
Tom Hanks is on an island,
beard like a hobo,
eventually goes crazy and
starts screaming at a volley ball.
          "Wilson! Wilson!"
          You remember?
That film was depressing though, man.
His fiancée married another guy.
Never waited for him.
I couldn't figure that out.'
I want to say, *It's cos she thinks he's dead*.
Instead I say,
          'You convinced an inmate to take a shower?'

'Why didn't his fiancée ditch her husband?
Wouldn't you, if you loved someone?
I would.
I'd put love first, you know?'

'You convinced someone to shower.'

'Oh, Joe, you woulda done the same.
Hanks was starting to hum,
then they went and moved him next to me
cos they knew I'd talk that wacko down.'

The warden reappears with
a can of Sprite in his hands.
He puts it on the desk,
then looks at me for far too long.
I pretend I don't notice.

   He leaves.

Ed continues to talk and
I listen but can't help staring at the soda
   – a gift from the warden –
a thank you cos Ed was helpful.
'Give back the soda,' I say, stopping Ed mid-sentence.

'Huh?'

'I got work,' I lie.
'I'll send money for more sodas.
Don't drink that one.'

Ed holds the cold can to his forehead.
'It's just a drink, Joe.
Don't get silly.'

I pound the desk with my fist.
'It *isn't* just a drink.'

The guard in my room sucks her teeth.
'Cool down or you're done here.'

Ed taps on the glass. 'What's wrong, man?'

I take a deep breath.
'You did them a favour.
They know you're a decent guy
yet they got you locked up like a serial killer.
Why's Tom Hanks here?
He probably butchered his own mother.'

Ed shrugs.
'They're doing a job, I guess.'
He opens the soda and gulps it down greedily.

'Yeah, well,' I say loudly,
for the benefit of the guard behind me,
'I wouldn't work here for a million bucks.'

Ed finishes the soda.
'You know, Joe,
you're made of stronger stuff
than most people.'

He looks at me
like he can really see me.
But he doesn't know me at all.
If he did, he'd see how much I hate this,
how little more I can take,
how much I need Angela here
or even Aunt Karen.
The only thing I've got is Nell.
And I haven't got her like I want her.
'The soda was a pay-off,' I say.

Ed won't argue.
'Mr Miller knows a soda isn't saving his soul.'

'He knows you're a good guy.'

'Am I?' Ed scratches his head.
'I didn't gun down a cop,
but I'm not a thoroughbred good guy.
I'm just ploughing through.

It's all any of us can do, right?
Even the warden.'

'Some people have power,' I say.

'We all have power, Joe.
Just gotta know how to use it, man.'

I don't know what he means
but I can't ask cos the guard calls time.

Power?
I can't even pay for a soda.

BROKEN

Death row is a place for broken people
      just like Tom Hanks.
They can't be fixed,
warped all out of shape
by the cracks and splinters inside them.

And what else can you do with stuff that's broken
except throw it into the trash?

      Right?

THE APARTMENT

The apartment was gross when I rented it:
        bugs everywhere,
        sticky floors,
        stained carpets.

But now Nell is visiting for breakfast
        I do what I can:
        clean the countertops,
        stick some frozen bagels into the oven
        to mask the smell;
        wipe down the sink with a dirty sock.
I do my best and still the place stinks,
not somewhere I want to be with Nell.

She knocks and I open the door,
planning to take her elsewhere.
        She pushes straight past me.
'I need the bathroom,' she says.

I point down the hall and she disappears,
runs the water
so I can't hear her pee.

And she comes back smiling.
'I was bursting.
Shouldn't have had a gallon of juice.
So this is your place.'
She stands in front of me,
puts a hand on my chest. 'You OK?'

I nod. My heart pounds under her hand.

'Can I tell you something?' she asks.

I nod again. My heart pounds harder.

'I only came over for one thing,' she says.

LIKE HELLFIRE

The longer I stand there, the fewer words I have.
But speechless never happens when I'm with a girl.
    Like *ever*.
I don't have a lot going for me,
but I know how to talk to girls,
get them to like me.

Nell smiles.
It makes me want to
        press her
        against the wall,
kiss her until neither of us can breathe.

But I don't do this.
I just stand staring,
happy to know she trusts me.

'Holy crap. Have you gone *shy*?' she asks.

I don't wait any more.
I put my hands behind her head,
pull her to me
and kiss her,
mouth open,
heart hammering like hellfire.

KISSING

Who knew kissing could feel so good?
Nell's lips, tongue, taste.
Gentle sips of her,
then great big gulps.
Her breath on my neck and
one word
in her mouth repeated over and over:
'Joe. Joe. Joe. Joe.'

It was everything.

And when she left, I didn't go for a run.

I didn't need to run anywhere.

TURN OVER

Sue disappears from the window without waving.
She doesn't come out with food either.
I'm about to go into the diner,
check everything's OK,
      when,
for no good reason,
I slip the key into the ignition.

And the car turns over.

First time.
No sputtering.

Nothing but the colicky purr of an engine
      sucking on dregs of gas.

'What the hell?' I say aloud.
Yesterday the crap heap wouldn't hiss,
now it's purring?
Was it the oil change? The battery?
It doesn't seem likely.
But what does it matter?
It's fixed!

Joy shoots through me
cos now I've got a job
and if Bob doesn't mind,
a car to see Ed in the afternoons
instead of walking and
baking my ass to a crisp.

Nell comes running. 'You got it working?'
She pounds her fist on the hood, screams.
'Sue, get out here! Sue!'

Sue plods down the steps,
stands next to Nell, hands on her hips.
'I hope Bob still needs a delivery guy,' she says,
        and winks,
        kidding,
        but it worries me
        because it's been an age since
        Bob talked about the job
        and it's not like I'll be in town
        for much longer.
Sue taps the licence plate with her toe,
then heads back towards the diner.
        I watch her go, a slow, fragile step,
        but Sue's not fragile.
        She's tough,
        cunning.

And I know she did this,
fixed the car while I slept or
got her boyfriend to do it.

But I won't ask anyone how it happened.
I'll accept it and pretend this miracle
had something to do with me.

GO HOME

Sue is wiping tables with a grey dishrag.
I scan the restaurant. 'Where's Nell?'
I've poured a lug of gas into the car,
hosed it down and cleaned it out.
Despite the lumpy tyres and rattling exhaust,
I'm taking the car for a ride. Nell too.

'In the bathroom,' Sue says.

Her eyes are red. But they weren't this morning.
    I take a step backwards.
'Everything OK?'

'Oh, you know,' Sue says.
She picks a chocolate chip from a muffin,
pops it into her mouth and
    slides the plate across the counter
    to me.
'It's my kid's anniversary.
He was a lifer at the farm.
Got knifed in a fight.
No one went down for it.
All lifers in his block,
so I guess it didn't matter much.'

She pulls out a packet of cigarettes,
unpeels the cellophane.
'Listen, Joe,
you stay for as long as Ed needs you
but then go home.
I came here for Jason
and I ain't never left.
Not even after he died,
and now I'm going nowhere.
They might as well have locked me up.
It's different for someone like Nell.
Her family's got a good reason to be here.'

Just then Nell appears, wiping wet hands on her shorts.
'Stupid hand dryer.
When's Bob gonna get a new one?'

'I'll leave you guys to it,' Sue says,
and scuttles into the kitchen.

Nell leans towards me.
'So, you taking me for a ride?'

A JOB

The car lurches and grinds its way out of Wakeling.
'You're gonna spend half your time
        pushing this crap heap around,' Nell says.

But I don't care.
        It's a car.
        Wheels.
I have a job.
For a few weeks anyway.

Until Ed no longer needs me
        in Texas.

MARRY ME

Ed uses his fingertips to flatten out his eyebrows.
'I got another marriage proposal in the mail.
Obviously on account of my looks.'

'What are you talking about?'

'Women think I'm the atom bomb, Joe.
Didn't you know?
I've been propositioned twenty-eight times
since I got locked up.'

'You're kidding.'

He holds up his palms:
I can see a mark in the middle of one,
like the remnants of a cigarette burn.
'Women are out of their sycamore trees.
They *love* the idea of hooking up with a guy behind bars.
No way I'm nailing her best friend if I'm
in here, right?
You know,
Johnny Vinzano got a proposal and that guy
did something so skanky it'd give
Charles Manson nightmares.'

'I don't get it,' I say.

'No one gets it.
But plenty of guys say yes.
Pete Browne married a girl from Utah last year.
She visits him every month.
Thing is, everyone knows Pete's gonna fry
cos he's full-blown guilty of
murdering his mother-in-law.'

'Do they get to … do the business?' I ask.

Ed bangs the table and laughs.
'No sex in here, man.
You're not even allowed to do yourself,
and that's the truth!
Guards catch you with your hands in your pants,
you're getting solitary.'
He pauses.
'You got a girl back home?'

I shake my head, think of Nell,
her face, clumpy walk,
bossy voice and the way she kisses –
slowly then quick,
like she's hungry.

And I consider telling Ed about her,
but pity stops me – or guilt.

'I think that's what I regret,' he says.
'That I never fell in love.
Maybe I'll marry that girl who wrote me after all.'

We spend the rest of the time determining
how we'd pick a wife,
getting no further than talking about
Catwoman.

And at the end
Ed, still laughing, says,
'How many days left?
I haven't looked at the calendar.'

It's twenty days
– twenty –
but I pretend I don't know either.
'Time's measured in moments, man,' I say instead.

MONMOUTH BEACH

It was fall.
The ocean was grey, not blue,
waves cannonballing on to the beach.
Mom, Angela and I were sitting on a blanket
eating peanut-butter-and-jelly bagels.
Ed was skimming stones into the sea,
his back to us.
Mom said,
　　　'Why the hell doesn't he just sit down?'

It wasn't a question.
She was irritated.
Always irritated by Ed,
like he was her annoying boyfriend
and not a son she should love.

I went to him,
　　　over the lumpy sand.

'That's Europe,' Ed said, pointing to the horizon.
'Wouldn't it be great to live over there?'

'Where?' I asked.

'Across the ocean,' Ed said.

I looked down at the sand for stones
to skim
but couldn't see any,
just washed-up water bottles,
cigarette butts,
candy wrappers.
My sneakers had a hole in the toe.

'Would you come with me?' he asked.
'If I got a job in London or Paris?
It would be mad exciting.
We could see Buckingham Palace
or the Eiffel Tower.
Europe has history, man.
It's got buildings older than this country!'

I spotted a small coral-coloured shell and
          picked it up.
'I'd go anywhere with you,' I told him.
And I meant it.

But when the time came,
he took off without me.
And he never made it anywhere near Europe,
never got across the Atlantic.

Yet here I am,
with him
like I promised.

DELIVERY BOY

It isn't hard to navigate Wakeling's grid system,
and after a couple days delivering
grilled cheese sandwiches,
I know my way around the whole town.
And I drive by Nell's house whenever I can:
I slow
           and search the windows for light.

I search for her.

BOTCHED

They botched an execution
in Louisana last night.
The guy on the gurney
didn't
get the proper anaesthetic,
wasn't even out cold
when they poisoned him
with potassium chloride
and he died of a massive heart attack.

It took Anthony Cruz, forty-six years old,
fifty-two minutes to die,
a vein in his neck bulging like a golf ball
where the nurse stuck in
the IV.
He was jerking, foaming from the mouth,
looked so horrific
they had to close the viewing gallery curtain
to stop anyone witnessing it.

That's the second botched execution
this month.

Shouldn't they let Ed live
until they figure it out?
The governor of Texas says
he doesn't think so.

DAY TRIP

'You wanna see some nature?' Nell asks.
She's figured out the best route to the
Davy Crockett National Forest.
'I promise you'll be at the prison by two.'

'Only if you got a playlist put together
for the ride,' I say, my face serious.

She waves her phone at me. 'Oh, *please*.
Think of this less as a drive,
more as an education,
or a musical cleansing, if you will.'
She pinches my chin between her fingers,
                        pecks my lips.

'Go suck it,' I say, pushing her away
and putting the car into gear.

MONKEY BABIES

Nell strokes the nape of my neck.
'You want me so bad,' I say.

'Oh, really?'
She withdraws her hand.

'No. Keep it there,' I beg.
I take her wrist, make her limp hand paw my face.

She snatches her hand back,
hides it beneath her knee
and suddenly
I imagine Plexiglas between us.

I push on the gas. The car jolts forward.
The world outside smudges by.
'You know, I can't even shake Ed's hand,' I tell her.
'It's stupid.
It's not like I could smuggle in a rifle.'

'A guy called Harlow did some study and
figured out that when faced with
a choice,
monkey babies
always chose comfort over food.

254

We can survive without anything except …'
She stares out at a passing truck,
        a mattress tied to its roof.

'Love?' I ask.

She nods. 'Apparently.
We can survive without anything except love.'

NIGHTMARES

I'd wake up screaming or in a wet bed,
and Ed never said, 'Grow up, Joe,'
or got cross about being woken.

He'd pull back his blanket
and let me sleep next to him.
And when I did,
the nightmares and bedwetting went away.

THE LAKE

We spread our sweaters on a rock
overlooking a lake.
It's early. No one's on the water yet.
The sky is pink. The air smells of pine.
Nell offers me some cranberry trail mix
but I'm not hungry.
'Isn't it weird how two worlds
can sit so close together?' I say.

Nell puts her head on my shoulder.
'It's people who build grey fortresses,' she says,
understanding me completely.

'I wish there were a way –' I say.

A wet dog darts out of the forest,
barks up at us on our rock.
His tail wags.
'Come on, Max!' a voice calls,
and the dog bounds back into the forest.

A LITTLE WHILE

We get back to Wakeling early and
go to my apartment.
Nell takes my face in her hands,
kisses my cheeks.

       One.
       Then the other.

'I'm gonna stay a little while,' she says.

MEANING IT

Being with Nell knocks my head back,
makes my bones thrum,
my blood ring and boil up
until we are
        reaching, grabbing, smothering
        each other.
And skin to skin our aching bodies press
        to find a way in –
and I mean pressing, pressing, pressing.

And there's teeth brawling, hands clutching,
as we pour our way into each other
until everything stops,
gives way to soft kisses,
quiet breaths of friendship,
and I say,
'Are you OK?'
        and actually fucking mean it.

AFTERWARDS

We share a tall glass of milk.
And we doze.

AN EMAIL FROM AL

Dear Angela and Joe,

Got good news:
Supreme Court says 'Let's hear it!'
so we're going to DC August 15.
Here's hoping the federal judges
will be smarter than the ones in Texas.
We're getting there.
I'll be in touch …
Best,
Al Mitchell

THEY'LL HEAR IT

So the date is set
three days before the
scheduled execution,
which is cutting it a bit fine
in my view.

BE HAPPY

I do my best to focus
on Ed's eyes,
brain batting away images of Nell in her underwear.
'The highest court in the country will hear us out.
That's gotta be good,' he says.

I give him two thumbs up.

Ed squints. 'You OK, little brother?'

Be here, I tell myself.
For God's sake, be here while you still can.

He raps on the Plexiglas with his knuckles,
jiggles his eyebrows at me.
'Oh, I know that look.'

'Huh?'

'You in love, little brother?'

I examine my hands.

'I'm pleased for you, Joe.
Don't give up that stuff for me.
Don't give it up for anyone.
If you need to go back to Arlington
to see a girl,
            that's what you should do.'

'I don't need to go anywhere,' I say.
I want to hold him,
find out how he smells.
I want to say *thank you* and *sorry* and
Please don't leave me again.

'Be happy,' Ed says.
'It's your duty to me, man.'

THE WALKING DEAD

We are on Nell's sofa watching
The Walking Dead,
Nell insisting that Rick Grimes is the
        perfect man,
clutching her heart whenever he comes on screen.

'You know the actor's English, right?
And the English are horrible kissers,' I say.

She flutters her eyelashes.
'Not in my experience.'

A zombie rips out a girl's throat and
Nell screams,
        hides behind a cushion.
'I can't watch,' she says,
but then does,
as a woman with a baseball bat
bashes in the brains
        of a zombie.
The woman's face is spattered in blood.
She drops the baseball bat,
but looks totally unshaken by the massacre.

And that's when I start to cry.
Nell takes my hand,
strokes my fingers.

I say,
'I don't know why I'm crying. I'm not sad.'

       But I can't stop.

GRILLED CHEESE

We've paused the TV,
are grilling cheese sandwiches,
when a voice calls out from the front hall:
'Smells like dinner!'
There's a laugh – the sound of love in it.

Nell startles
like a cat facing an oncoming car,
a cat who knows her nine lives are up.
She tries to grab the sandwiches from the pan
with her bare hand,
burns her fingers.
She yelps.

I run the faucet,
drag her over by the wrist,
hold her hand under cold water.

'I'll go,' I whisper,
wondering how quickly I could unlock
the patio doors and be in the backyard,
gone so she doesn't get into trouble.
But why would she?
Isn't she allowed a boyfriend?
It's not like we're rolling naked on the rug.

Nell bites her trembling bottom lip.
'I should have said something.
I was going to, but I couldn't.'

And then he walks in,
       one arm swinging,
       face fixed into a smile.
       A smile that fades
       when he sees me with his daughter.
       'Joseph Moon,' he says evenly.

'Warden,' I reply.

'Oh God. Oh God, I'm so sorry,' Nell stammers.

DUEL

The warden eyeballs me
like we're about to duel.
He waits for me to make the first move.
I don't.
And neither does he.

Nell is shaking.
And why wouldn't she?
'You lied,' I say,
            turning to her,
            turning *on* her,
            my tone toxic.
Roughly I let go of her wrist,
move closer to the patio doors.

The warden pulls up his pants by the waistband,
            takes two
            long strides towards Nell,
                        stands in front of her making
                        himself into a wall between us.
'What are you doing here, Joseph?' he asks.

'Me? Oh, I was deciding whether to steal
your blender, desk lamp
or daughter.'

Nell flinches.
'Joe's a friend. I can explain.'
And maybe she tries,
but I don't wait around to hear it.

'Don't go, Joe!' Nell shouts. 'Joe!'

I step into the darkness,
her voice behind me calling.

ANOTHER PICTURE MESSAGE

From Reed.
A photo of a girl in a bikini this time,
thin with tan skin
and a grin that says,
My worries are elsewhere.
She is holding an ice cream cone;
her flip-flops are red.
Usually I'd confirm she's hot,
say Reed's one lucky bastard
and ask for more pictures.

But I don't feel like it tonight.

A REMINDER

'Aunt Karen's been at the house
spouting about how psychologically damaging
seeing Ed will be,' Angela says.
'She's, like, genuinely concerned
for both of us.'

I haven't the patience for Angela's excuses,
her *I'm coming soon* promises.
'Are you flying down or not?
Cos in case you didn't know,
time's running out.
The execution is in fourteen days.'

'Yeah, Joe, I know that,
but thanks for reminding me what an
asshole I am.'

FIREWORKS

My first Fourth of July without Ed,
and the whole island was at Fort Wadsworth
watching the fireworks.
Angela chewed on a liquorice lace,
one arm around me.
Aunt Karen pointed into the sky
at every burst of colour,
every whizz and bang.
Mom wasn't with us.
'She's not well,' Aunt Karen told me.
I knew it wasn't true.
I'd seen Mom getting ready to go out
through the keyhole of her bedroom.
Aunt Karen
did that:
          protected us from Mom's lies,
          from knowing about her dates with losers
          or when she got drunk.
But I knew the truth.
Looking back now I know
I only ever pretended to be persuaded.

A MISTAKE

I push past Nell to get into the diner,
but more roughly than I mean to
and she stumbles,
grabs the handrail.

'Shout at me then,' she says,
       following me inside.

Sue is stirring a hot pot of oatmeal.
       Seeing us, she slides into the kitchen.

Nell puts her hand over the bags ready for delivery.
'Tell me what I was meant to do once I knew.'

'You could have talked to me,'
I say through clenched teeth.

'I talk to you more than to anyone, Joe.
My whole life I've just been Miller's kid.
       A spoilt, surly bitch,
       the kid whose dad kills for a living.
With you, I wasn't,
and when that happened
I didn't want to be his daughter any more,

especially not around you
cos of everything it meant.
You'd have hated me.'
She is screeching.

'We can't be friends now.
I've too much to think about,' I tell her.

'You don't mean that.'

'I do. Please leave me alone, Nell.'

'Whatever,' she says,
and rushes out of the diner by the back door.

I'm breathing heavily. My heart is thumping.

Sue reappears looking flustered.
She must have heard everything.
'You're making a mistake letting her leave,' she says.

I DON'T KNOW WHY

I don't know why I didn't
put my arms around her,
tell her it's OK,
that I know she never meant to hurt me,
that sometimes we like people we shouldn't
and by the time we feel
what we feel
it's already too late.

NO REHEARSAL

I arrive at the prison early, sit sweating in the car,
      waiting.
Father Matthew taps on the windshield.
'Time for a beverage today?' he asks.

He sits opposite me in the visitors' room,
sips at a peppermint tea.
He's wearing a lemon-coloured shirt
      buttoned up to the neck,
         baggy brown pants with more pockets
         than any ordinary person needs.
And he's younger than I remember –
grey hair adding years to his life that aren't there.
He's definitely no older than forty.
'Ed tells me you got a job,' he says.
'Wakeling ain't heaving with opportunity.
I reckon you done good.'
The priest studies me like you might
a painting in a museum,
checking my face for revealing cracks and bumps.
'I do believe you got something on your mind.'

'I'm fine.'
I'm not sure why I agreed to sit
with the priest in the first place.

Was I planning a confession?
Did I want to tell him how I've treated Nell?
Maybe I should explain I can't do what Ed's asked:
     I can't be happy.
     I don't know how,
          especially not now.

He rolls a paper napkin into a ball.
'I been watching you coming and going, Joe.
All that's in mind, when I see you, is respect.'
He grins.
Is he mocking me?
'I mean to say, I admire you.
You coulda stayed in New York,
come down just before August eighteenth.
Or you coulda come down and skipped visits.
You haven't.
You've walked miles in mugginess,
and though I reckon you been
quietly
grumbling and grousing,
your brother don't know how tough it is.
Ed talks to me, see.'
He scratches the bridge of his nose.
'You, Joe, leave the complaining at home.'

We sit in silence for a minute.
Then I ask, 'Will he die, Father?'

'We're all dying.
And in some ways they killed part of him already.'

'I'm living in a parallel universe.'

Father Matthew reaches across the table and
tries to take my hand.
Instinctively
        I pull it away.
        He doesn't react.
'You stay in today, Joe,
cos tomorrow's a story that ain't been written yet.
No use in rehearsing it.
No use at all.'

A couple at another table laugh,
forgetting where they are, I guess.

'It's two o'clock,' I tell him.
'I gotta go.'

POKER

'Don't you ever miss Mom?' I ask Ed.
He concentrates on my face.
'No,' he says. 'Do you?'

'Not usually. But I wonder why not.
Does that make me cold?'

Ed holds up a hand to stop me speaking.
'Hey. Think about it this way.
If you're playing poker
and you never get any good cards,
you might think,

> *Damn, I put so much money into this game,*
> *I gotta keep going cos*
> *eventually I'll get thrown an ace of hearts,*

you know?
But I don't think about poker like that.
Makes no sense to keep betting on a losing game.
Cut your losses.
Run out of that casino and
  spend your cash on a martini.'

I must look confused.

'It's the same with people,' he explains.
'You keep placing bets on someone
who never comes through,
you're just a total nutcracker.
Put your money on a sure bet.
Or a better bet, at least.'

'Mom might visit.
She might be the ace of hearts that comes through.'

Ed throws his hands in the air.
'Then let her come. But I sure as hell
won't be putting any money on it.'

SID SIPS

'*Sid sips from it*,' I read aloud real slowly,
sounding out each letter,
     each word,
          before I could understand the
          sentence.

Angela patted my hand, jiggled me
up and down
on her lap.
'Nice job,' she said.

Ed wasn't a book person.
He watched from the couch
making faces,
     making us laugh,
          making my homework take
          forever.

Angela said, 'Keep going, Joe.
Don't you wanna know what Sid did next?'

Ed smirked. 'Did he stick his finger up his ass?'

Angela threw an eraser across the room,
hit Ed on the side of the head with it.

'You are *not* helping!' she shouted.

Mom burst in from the kitchen.
'Keep the noise down,
I'm trying to take a call for God's sake.'

'Joe can read,' Angela said.
She held up the book,
waved it so Mom wouldn't miss it.

'That's great, Angela.
Once you're done teaching Joe,
have a go with Ed, huh?
Maybe if he learns to read he'll get a job
and stop sponging off his mother.'

Ed opened his mouth to say something
but for the first time
didn't answer back.
It was like
he was trying to understand something new.

'She didn't mean it,' Angela said.

Ed blinked. 'Oh, I think she did.'

SPECIAL PROVISIONS

The farm sends a letter:
they've made special provisions for prison visits
in the run up to August 18.
The week before,
a meeting room will be available
to allow
full contact
visits with Ed,
and on the day
prior to execution,
visiting hours will be
      extended
      for family members,
      a spiritual adviser
      and one legal representative.

The letter suggests that if
I have questions I should contact
Philip Miller directly.

I have questions,
but none he could answer.

LIGHTENING

I drop off a hundred dollars' worth of pies
     and my phone rings.
It isn't Nell.
It's Angela.
I haven't the energy to talk.
I answer anyway.
     'I'm flying to Houston tomorrow,' she cheeps.
     'Bus into Wakeling three hours later!'

'Really? That's awesome.'
She isn't coming so we can see the rodeo but still …
She can visit the prison too.
I won't be alone in the apartment.
Someone can share this load,
     which is already lifting
          a bit
          with the news.

'Thank God you're coming,' I tell her.

'Tomorrow.'

DRAFT

I draft a message to Nell on my phone.
But I don't send it;
I change my mind and
      delete the whole thing.

I miss her, but I can't send any message.

Why not?

I mean,
      why the hell not?

LUGGAGE

Angela is thin,
hair flat and dirty,
a weakened smile.

She waves lightly,
letting go of the handrail and
slipping down the bus steps.

      I catch her at the bottom.

She's shaking like she'll
collapse if I let go.

The bus driver cracks open the undercarriage,
wrestles with suitcases,
grunting and shunting
      bags on to the sidewalk like garbage.

'Did you bring luggage?' I ask Angela.
She laughs so hard the sound
fills the station.
People look.

'I did. I brought luggage,' she tells me
and presses her face into my neck.

CLOSER TO HOME

Angela puts her purse on the floor,
then quickly picks it up again.

Our house in Staten Island is small,
the neighbourhood grotty,
but our place was always clean.
Aunt Karen saw to that.

'I'm sorry it isn't nicer,' I say.

'I expected worse,' she says.

We lean against the countertop.
'Thanks for the money,' she says.
        'What money?' I ask.
        'The money you sent.'
        'I didn't send you money, Ange.'
        She frowns. 'You didn't?'
        'No.'

She gazes at a brown stain on the lino,
looks like she's working through every problem
that ever existed in her mind
all at the same time.

'Mom called Ed,' I say.

'What for?' she asks.

I shrug.

> Angela shakes her head and
> goes to the bathroom,
> slamming the door closed.

The extractor fan whirrs and crackles,
water splashes from the taps.
>   This is noise
>   in my apartment that isn't me.
And it makes me feel a little closer to home.

NOW

Now I've got Angela
I shouldn't miss Nell so much.
I shouldn't think about her.
But I do.
In the mornings I still
check my phone for messages
before my eyes have opened.
At night I sleep early
to stop myself waiting for her call.

I should focus on my job,
my brother,
on why I'm here in the first place.

I shouldn't be fixated on Nell.
She isn't who I thought she was.

And anyway, she was a time filler,
a way to keep my mind off Ed.

I used her to tread water.

Isn't that all it was?

EVA

Angela plays Eva Cassidy through a Bluetooth speaker,
again and again,
'Autumn Leaves' and 'Over the Rainbow',
songs so sad I can barely listen.
'Cassidy died when she was thirty-three,'
Angela informs me.
'Tried to fight her cancer but couldn't.
Her last performance was "What a Wonderful World"
for family and friends.'

'Why are you telling me this?' I ask.

'I don't know,' she says.
'Just makes you think.'

'About death.'

'About life. How little we're promised,' she says,
and turns up the music.

A HOLDING BAY

The night before her first prison visit Angela asks,
'What's it like?'

'Like limbo,
a place where nothing lives,
a holding bay,' I say.

She twirls her hair around her fingers
                                    tirelessly.

ANGELA'S FIRST VISIT

Instead of running a metal detector
down my body and
            waving me through
                    as they usually do,
a guard gestures for me to follow and a
female guard accompanies Angela.

I'm taken to an office. The guard closes the door.
'I need you to strip.'

'Sorry?' I don't know the guard.
Maybe he's new and
doesn't understand Section A regulations.
'I need to search you before the contact visit.'

I flatten my back against the door.
I know what a strip search means,
how much of myself I'll have to expose.
'Did the warden approve this?' I ask.

He snaps a latex glove against his wrist
like he's in a goddamn movie.
Another guard comes in yawning –
a chaperone.

I glance at the wall clock.
It's already two minutes after two.
Ed will be waiting.

I can't make him wait.

REAL

It's a different room,
an ordinary room like a place you might meet
a school counsellor,
and no Plexiglas –
nothing to divide us.

Angela is already there with Ed,
arms around him,
hanging on as though he might
     float away
       like a helium balloon.

When they hear the door,
they look up,
see me standing next to the guard.

'My little brother,' Ed says,
      and I rush to him.

I hold on to him too.

He's real.

THE LAVENDER ROOM

Angela is definitely not a contender for
America's Got Talent.
She sings for Ed anyway,
getting the words to the songs wrong,
laughing when the melody is
> too high
>> for her to reach.

She sings stuff by Adele,
songs Ed doesn't know all that well.
Yet he grins the whole time.

And so do I.

Because being in this lavender room
with bars on its windows,
guards on both sides of the door,
> we are on the verge
> of being a family again.

'I missed you guys,' Ed says.

'You aren't ticked off that we didn't come
to Texas before all this?' I ask.

Ed claps me on the back.

'Life's too short for that crap, man.

Nah.

    We're together now.'

MAJOR-GENERAL

Ed was Major-General Stanley in his school
production of *The Pirates of Penzance*.
We had a video recording of it at home
we watched sometimes,
laughing so hard
at Ed singing
and at the haircut he had when he was thirteen.
Mom would come in
to investigate the noise.
'Oh, you're watching that again.
Haven't you seen it enough?'

'It's the Ed show,' I told her.

'Yeah. And I'm sort of wondering
when it'll be over.'

OUTSIDE THE PRISON

Nell's leaning against the car,
earphones in, head down.
She kicks at the dirt.
'What do you want?' I snap,
when all *I* want is to kiss her,
tell her I forgive her,
beg her to see me later –
        somewhere we can be alone.

But a stupid part of me wants to make her suffer,
        see if she'll fight for me.
        Am I worth an argument?

'I came to see my dad and saw your car,' she says.
'I decided to say sorry. Again.
Like it'll help.'

Angela wanders off without a word,
pokes at her phone.

'Your sister looks like you,' Nell says.
'She's pretty. But she needs some of Sue's
high calorie apple pie. You do too.'
She tries for a laugh.

'Come on …
        At least tell me to go to hell.'

'I don't want you to go to hell, Nell.'

She leans towards me. 'Tell me what I should do.
If you say you need me to leave you alone,
I'll understand.
I won't like it,
but I'll understand.'

'In a week, your dad will
stamp my brother off the face of the earth.'

'It's all he talks about, Joe.
He doesn't believe Ed's phony confession.
And he said there are a dozen scumbags who should've
got their dates before your brother.
But if Dad refuses to execute him, he'll lose his job.'

'And save Ed's life.'

She looks down at her grubby sneakers.
'For how long? An hour? A day?

You think they wouldn't replace my father in a
          heartbeat?
He isn't the one keeping him here.'

'He's part of the crooked system.
He's as much a murderer as any of
the guys on the row.'

'So what does that make me?
Guilty by association?'
She reaches for a stone,
wipes it clean on her shirt,
polishes it between her thumb and forefinger.
'Out of everyone, I thought you'd
understand how shitty that is.'

'You wanna meet later?' I ask.

She squints. 'Yes. I really do.'

HEALING

Nell is beside me in a booth
drinking hot chocolate and chatting with Angela
like they've known one another
                              forever.

It's no big deal.

Just sitting.

Talking and drinking.

But this helps me feel better.
Nell heals me.

And I've no idea how she does it.

PREPARATION

'They weighed me and took my measurements,'
Ed says.
'I mean, they fucking *weighed* me.'

Angela squeezes my knee
so I know this must signify something.
I try to figure out what he means.
I don't want him saying the bad stuff aloud.

Ed puffs out his cheeks.
'They gotta know how much drug to use.
And every dead guy needs a coffin, right?'

'They measured you for a coffin?' I ask slowly.

He ignores me. 'I don't really get it.
Why not just use a truckload of poison
for everyone?
If we overdose, who cares?
Dead is dead.'

Angela pulls her chair next to Ed's.
'It's *not* gonna happen,' she tells him.

'They moved me to the end cell,' he murmurs.
'That's so I'm closer to the chamber.
And also so fewer people have to
walk by my cell every day.
You know the worst bit about it?'

       I can't even imagine.
       And part of me doesn't want to know.

'They made me carry my own mattress and
blanket and stuff.
They watched me do it and didn't help.
They watched me carry my bedding
to the last cell.'

       My mind is mud:
       nothing moves in it.
       What can I say to this?
       What possible comfort could any words have?

'It isn't fair,' Angela says.
She holds his chin,
forces him to look at her.
'It isn't fair,' she repeats.

NOT FAIR

It was a snow day.
Every school in the city closed
except mine.

'It's not fair!' I screamed,
still in my pyjamas.

'Oh, get over it! Life isn't fair!' Mom screamed back.
'Now get dressed.'

Ed walked me to school.
      We stomped fresh paths
      of boot prints through snow,
watched kids playing,
adults shovelling sidewalks,
snowploughs pushing away their snow hoards
      to God-knows-where.

Ed tied a knot in my scarf,
patted my head,
nudged me through the school gates.
'I'll collect you at two thirty,' he said.
'It's not fair,' I repeated.

'I know it isn't, little man,' he said.

'And I'm sorry.

But I promise I'll be here to pick you up.'

THE GALLERY

It's seven days until the scheduled execution
and Angela has Al Mitchell on speakerphone:
'Ed can have a family member or friend
sit in the gallery as a witness.
But Angela's the only one approved.
You have to be eighteen.
I get a seat and also Father Matthew.'

'She's invited to watch him die?' I ask.

He doesn't answer.
'A member of the victim's family has
requested a spot in the gallery.
The press would have places and
some of the prison staff.
My advice is don't take the seat.'

'Why would anyone watch?' I ask.

'I want to be there,' Angela says.
'I won't let him do it on his own
and there's nothing you can do
to change my mind.'

THE RETURN

Nell and I are lying on the sofa.
Angela's in the bedroom on the phone
but keeps calling out.
'You guys better be behaving.'
She hoots like it's the funniest joke ever,
goes back to whispering.

And the doorbell rings.
A jangle that makes Nell jump.
'Is it your dad?' I ask.

She shrugs. 'I hope not.'

I peer through the peephole.
        It's not Philip Miller.
        It's someone I never expected to see in Texas:
        it's Aunt Karen.

A MISTAKE

I don't tell Aunt Karen to leave or
slam the door in her face.
I don't shout at her for making me live
in hell for so long
when she had money to help.
I don't blame her for leaving
Ed here
for all these years
when he needed someone,
when he hadn't done anything wrong.
I say, 'You came,'
      and she nods.

WHAT CAN WE FORGIVE?

Anything.

> If that's what we choose.

TOO LATE

Aunt Karen takes her coffee light
with a lot of sugar.
I make it to her liking but she doesn't
even taste it.
She balances on the sofa,
absorbing her surroundings
and asking a hundred legal questions
which Angela and I haven't a clue how to answer.
We needed her to take an interest a month ago
or when Ed first got locked up.

It feels too late to fight now.

LAND OF THE FREE

Al Mitchell orders a cheesesteak sandwich from Sue,
opens his briefcase,
>   making a shield of one half,
>   ducking behind it,
>   shuffling through papers.

'So,
we have the Supreme Court
in three days,' he says loudly,
>   reappearing,
>   slamming it closed.

Angela sips at iced tea.
Aunt Karen frowns.
I listen.

'We have a solid case.
Anyone with two brain cells can see Ed's
a victim of circumstance.'

'How's that?' Aunt Karen asks steadily.
She didn't even order a water.

Al throws his shoulders back.

312

'Ed was convicted on a false confession
he made when he was eighteen,
tired, hungry and threatened.
Nothing else links him to the crime apart from a
run-in with Frank Pheelan hours earlier.
They haven't any witnesses,
no DNA.
It's laughable.'
Al grins
but not like he's encouraging anyone
to join him.

Angela exhales.
'Someone else did it,' she says.

Al narrows his eyes.
'Prosecutors told the jury his DNA was found
        in the cruiser.
        Which it was.
But they weren't told it was only found
        on his driver's licence,
which the cop had taken from him.'

Sue arrives with a steaming steak sandwich
and shuffles away again.

Al looks at it, grimaces,
taps his temples with his fingertips.
'It's reasonable doubt.'

'Have you *ever* convinced the Supreme Court?'
I ask.
I want him to admit what we all know,
forget all the lawyer-speak
and tell us the truth.

He looks me straight in the eye.
'The court ensures justice is done, Joe.'
And he wants me to believe it,
wants to believe it himself.
But how can he when he's been
representing guys like Ed forever?
                              He knows the deal.

I slide out of the booth, the diner,
            into the heat of the afternoon
            hating with every inch of my bones
            the so-called free country I live in,
            the home of the brave.

HOW DO YOU SAY GOODBYE?

I count down our time together
as soon as I sit,
one eye on Ed,
the other on the clock,
sometimes wishing Angela wouldn't sing
cos the songs take so long,
wishing Aunt Karen hadn't turned up to share
this time and space
which I want to
      myself
      now.

And in those final five minutes
while I'm waiting for the guard to tap his watch,
I never know how to sew up our time together,
                 make it count,
                 dilute the sadness.
Anger rises in my throat
and I leave with a rock of molten rage
      burning up my guts.

Angela, Karen and I don't talk on the way out;
we walk side by side,

but I always feel totally alone
trying to figure out
how the hell I'll ever say goodbye for good.

REMOVAL

Philip Miller sends a letter
reminding us to make arrangements
for the removal of Ed's body
after execution.

>He vouches for Vander & Sons
>on Wakeling's Main Street.

I hand the letter to Aunt Karen.
'You wanna help?
Deal with this,' I tell her.

Because I can't do it.

PLANNING

A neighbour in Arlington had diabetes
that did her in last December.
I'd never seen so many flowers,
lilies that stank up the church.

Angela's friend Susie-May died
in a car accident on her way home from Montauk.
She was tanned,
newly engaged.
Everyone said she would've made a great hairdresser.

But it happens, doesn't it?
    Death.
Either suddenly or steadily.

But you never put it on your calendar,
    X marks the spot –
        let's get the headstone in a Black Friday sale
        and have the name chiselled into it.

You can never usually plan on death like that.

A CHANCE

In a pocket of silence
between greedy
bites
of jelly doughnuts
in Wakeling's strip mall parking lot,
Nell says,
  'Dad thinks Ed has a chance in
   DC tomorrow
  at the Supreme Court.'

'Really?' I ask.

It's raining heavily for the first time since
I arrived,
washing all the humidity out of the air.
The car's wipers swish
  back and forth.

'Yeah,' she says,
  so what do I do?
  I start to
  get my hopes up.

HOPE

It's the hope that'll kill you.

UNITED STATES SUPREME COURT ORDER

(ORDER LIST: 576 US)

AUGUST 15, 2016

CERTIORARI DENIED

15-6898
(15A6644)

MOON, EDWARD R.V. COMMISSIONER, TX DOC. ET AL.

The application for stay of execution of sentence
of death presented to Justice Williams and by him
referred to the Court is denied. The petition for a
writ of certiorari is denied.

THE WRIT

So.
I guess that's it.
The Supreme Court have denied Ed's appeal.

GET OUT

Angela is in her bed shirt,
hair piled on top of her head,
eyes ringed with black make-up.
'The lawyers *always* have final appeals.
I've seen documentaries. I'll call Al,'
Angela says.
She rummages in her purse
then turns it upside down,
the entire contents chaotically spilling on to the
                                    unmade bed.
She grabs her phone,
        scrolls through it.

Ed's only hope now is Heath McDowell and
there's little chance of the Texas governor
showing leniency towards a convicted cop killer –
        not when he's up for re-election.
And yet I say, 'It's gonna be OK,' cos
it's what Angela needs to hear.

Suddenly
she swings for me
        like a feral cat.
'Get out!' she shouts. 'I don't need your horse shit.'

'Angela.'

'Get *out*!' she screams.

I leave,
        closing the door gently behind me,
                while Angela smashes up the bedroom.

MORNING RUN

I keep my eyes firmly fixed ahead,
    don't look
    left or right,
        hammer the cement with my feet,
        pummel my way through town
running faster, faster, faster.
If this were a race
it would be my personal best.
I can feel it without checking my watch for timings.

And at Nell's, I stop,
    morning sweat
    dripping from the end of my nose.
I call. She picks up after two rings.
'The Supreme Court said no,' I tell her.
'I'm outside. I need to see your dad.'

Her bedroom blinds open
    from the bottom
        up.
She is at the window in a purple vest,
    one strap down at the shoulder.
'I'll wake him,' she says.

HUDDLE

Philip Miller isn't wearing any shoes
and it makes him seem vulnerable,
with those very old white feet.
He sits opposite me, at the table,
          hands clasped.

Nell puts a plate of cookies between us,
                    two mugs and a coffee pot.
'I'll go get ready,' she says, and rushes away.

The warden
      pours himself a large, steaming mug of coffee.

I hold my head in my hands.
'I've no idea why I'm here,' I say,
staying where I am cos Ed needs help
and I don't know who else to ask;
Nell's dad is the only person I know with power.
'Washington denied our appeal,' I tell him.

He nods. 'I got a message. I'm very sorry.'
His eyes are bloodshot;

I'm sure he'd go back to bed, if given the option.
But I guess he's going to be kept pretty busy now.

'Can you predict which guys will get a call
from the governor?' I ask.

He frowns. 'No. A stay of execution
happens for so many reasons.'

'Like what?'

He brushes his hands through his hair.
He doesn't want to do this,
explain the process or give me any insight into the
unpredictability of it –
       the randomness.
'A few years ago a guy called Neil Huddle
set fire to his house and killed his
wife and kids for insurance money.
You know how much?
       Sixty thousand bucks.
That's what his family were worth.
There was so much evidence against Huddle,
his own mother said he was guilty.
But two hours beforehand the governor
called me up,

told me to pull the brakes because Huddle's lawyers
proved he was crazy.'
　　　He pauses.
'I mean, you kill your family for peanuts,
I'd say you're a few peppermint creams
short of a Christmas box.'

'So he got off?'
　　　Should Al put forward this case for Ed?
　　　Could we say it's unnatural to be so calm
　　　　　　about your own death?
　　　Or maybe I could convince Ed to
　　　attack a guard or eat his own crap.
　　　It would be a long shot,
　　　　　　but that's the stage we're at.

'I had to send him to a top-security mental hospital
so he could get better,' Philip Miller says.
'And he did. They said they
made him *not crazy* any more
then sent him back to us for execution.'
He is talking quickly, angrily.

I wait a moment
　　　to summon up some courage.
　　　'And can *you* stop it?

If you called the governor and explained
that Ed's a good guy
and doesn't deserve death?'

'What do *you* think, Joseph?'
He holds my gaze
and I want to hate him
but I can see he isn't proud of his power.

'No one ate the cookies,' Nell says.
She looks at us anxiously.

'I gotta go be with my family,' I say, and stand,
then sprint away
as I did the last time I was here.

I don't stop running
until I'm back at the apartment.

NOSY PEPPERS

Ed knows about the Supreme Court decision,
smiles anyway and says,
'Let's make the best of our last couple days.'
And we try.
We rag on each other,
tell stories from when we were kids.

Then
Ed turns to one of the guards and asks,
        'What does a nosy pepper do?'

She searches for a serious answer.
        'I don't know, Edward.'

        'It gets jalapeño business,' he says,
            and laughs from the pit of his tummy,
which makes me laugh
and Angela
and even Aunt Karen.

After a couple of minutes the guard snorts.
        'Jalapeño business. Oh, OK, I get it.'

JOKES

'Knock-knock,' Ed said.
'Who's there?' I asked.
'Moo.'
'Moo who?'
'Cows don't say who, they say moo.'
Ed tittered
      while I fell
      on to the rug laughing.
I was four.
I couldn't tell my own jokes,
only laugh at Ed's.
But I tried.
'Knock-knock,' I said.
'Who's there?' Ed asked.
'Moo.'
'Moo who?'
'Moo-boo-too-loo!' I told him.
I laughed. Clapped my hands.
      Ed rolled his eyes.
'Not quite,' he said. 'You gotta have a punchline.
Like, a bit that makes people laugh cos
you've been clever with your words.'

'I got smarts,' I announced.
'You're a smart*ass*, you mean,' he said and
patted my head.

I chewed my sweater cuff,
tried to figure out what made Ed's joke funny,
my joke lame.

And then I said, 'Knock-knock.'
'Who's there?'
'Ghost.'
'Ghost who?'
'Ghosts don't say who, they say BOO!'

Ed winced as I screamed the punchline at him,
then put up a hand for me to high-five.
'Now we're cooking, little man,' he said.
'Hell, that joke was better than mine!'

THE VIGIL

Candles and poster boards held high,
hymns and prayers mumbled
into the night air.
'That's for Ed,' Al says,
meeting us as we leave the prison
and stating the obvious.
These are Ed's supporters,
people who don't want my brother to die,
gathering around the prison like the survivors
of an apocalypse.
'They come every time.
And they'll be here until the end.'

The End:
the words burn
and I have to
        rest my hands on my knees to stop myself
        falling over.

Angela rubs my back.
'Let's go,' she says. 'Tomorrow will be a long day.'
But it won't.

August 17 will
        come and
        be gone again
before we've had time to do
        anything
        that will ever matter.

WHEN YOU KNOW BETTER

Aunt Karen doesn't get into my space much,
sleeps next to Angela and only speaks
when she's asked for her opinion.
But tonight she's in the kitchen baking
cinnamon buns,
the smell
      swelling up the apartment with a feeling
of family,
which I'm sure it's never known before.

Angela sits on the floor in the sitting room,
piles of papers around her,
trying to
find a loophole somewhere,
a way to
postpone
what is speeding
towards us
like an unstoppable freight train.

'Anyone hungry?' Aunt Karen asks.
Her skin is grey,
her hair so thin and white
she's turned into an old lady.

I go to her.
'Don't feel guilty any more.
You're here. It's more than Mom's managed.'

'Guilt would be easy,' she says.
'Guilt would be about what I've done.
But it's shame I feel, Joe.
Shame that what I've done is
a reflection of who I am.
Who *am* I?'

Angela joins us.
'You were an aunt doing her best.'

'It wasn't good enough,' Karen says.

Angela elbows her tenderly.
'Hey, when you know better, you do better.'

The oven begins to beep.
It beeps and beeps.
The cinnamon buns have baked.

I DREAM

Kids in camouflage sprint and stumble through smoke,
their faces smeared with blood and dirt.
It's a burnt-out city with kids tearing into enemy lines,
no weapons,
scrabbling around in torn vests looking for
bits of paper
                    to use as shields.

The guerrillas aren't interested in words,
don't care how young the soldiers are,
that most couldn't grow beards.
They pull out machetes, slice right into them,
        these boys,
leaving them
bleeding to death on the ground.

And in the background,
a diner's broken neon sign
flashes ceaselessly.

LAST DAY

I   wake before five.
I   can't get back to sleep.
I   clock-watch,
flicking through photos of Nell on my phone.
She is scowling in each one.
I haven't any of Ed –
they won't let me bring my phone in.

Angela wanders into the living room in the dark
and then we are sitting
side by side on the
blow-up bed,
watching out the window,
Ed's last sunrise,
a poppy-red sky he can't see from his cell.

        'We can do this,' Angela says.
        'Can we?' I ask.
        'We have to,' she reminds me.

NEED

Nell arrives at ten o'clock with a lasagne.
'Sue said you have to eat.'
I put the dish into the refrigerator.
'I can stay or leave. Whatever you need,' Nell says.

'I need to buy milk and toilet paper,' I tell her.

It's close to a hundred degrees,
the air hazy with humidity.
At the convenience store I put
milk, Pepsi and toilet paper into the basket.
Then I slip some hard candy
into the pocket of my shorts.
I have an urge to steal,
take something that doesn't belong to me.

At the counter, Nell wraps her arm around my waist.
'Do you want company later?
I can wait for you outside the farm.'

'Definitely,' I say. 'I need you.'
As I say it, I realise it's true.

'I need you too,' she says.

READY

Angela, Karen and I scrape around the apartment,
                heat up
                squares of lasagne
                we never eat,
and check our phones for updates,
the TV for news that never comes.

Nothing changes.
And all day long,
while we tread water,
the farm is getting ready –
filling needles,
checking straps,
rehearsing their parts like actors in a play
so everyone knows what to do,
won't miss a cue
and mess up the whole operation.

I guess that by now
they're pretty much ready.

AMAZING GRACE

The protesters sing outside the prison,
giving Ed a voice.
It's well meant
but too late.
He needed support during his trial
and the early appeals.

They're just here for the night,
the countdown,

cos this is what they do;
it doesn't matter to them who's for the gurney
or whether they're guilty or not.

They notice us drive in, wave cautiously.
I wave back my weak-willed appreciation.
Maybe, afterwards, I should join them –
sing a couple of verses of 'Amazing Grace'.
What harm could it do?

But not now.
Now it's time to see Ed.

The last time.

It is too soon.

THE LAST SUPPER

Ed rushes at us and
     a guard reaches with his arms to stop him,
     but thinks better of it,
     allows
     the four of us to stand in a
     tight huddle.
Ed smells sour – like he hasn't showered in days,
but I don't let go.
I breathe him in until he unpeels himself
from us,
waves towards a table.
'KFC!' he announces.
'I told them I didn't want anything special,
but the warden ordered this anyway.
Chicken, fries, coleslaw, potato salad.
Looks good, right?'
He drums the air with his hands.
'And what made me happiest of all …'
He points to a bucket filled to the brim
with cans of Dr Pepper.
'Soda!' he shouts.

'You'll spend all day in the bathroom,' Aunt Karen says,
crossing her legs,

pawing the gold crucifix
hanging around her neck.
'Thank goodness,' she says,
touching an electric fan next to her which
is slowly whisking hot air around the room.

At the table,
Ed fills a plate with food and
brings it to Angela. 'Wanna drink?'

'You eat it.
We'll get something later,' she says.

Ed shakes his head.
'I want us to eat together.
A last supper.
You can pretend I'm Jesus.'

The guard laughs, but not unkindly.

Ed turns to him.
'You want something to gnaw on, John?' he asks.
'You haven't had lunch yet.'

'No, Ed. I'm good. You dig in.'

Ed fills a second plate,
hands it to Aunt Karen,
then another for me.

I stare at the food on my lap.
How will I force it into my mouth?

Ed fills his own plate and sits next to me,
hands me a can of Dr Pepper.
'This is nice,' he says. 'Right?'

I try for a smile
cos Ed's right – it is nice
not spending our last hours
        fenced off from each other
        by Plexiglas.
But I can think of better days
                we've had
                together.

LIBERTY STATE PARK

It was spring.
Ed was fifteen.
I was five.
Angela had made
a lopsided spongecake
with Reese's Pieces stuck into the cream frosting.
Aunt Karen brought a bag of cold burgers.
Mom was wearing sunglasses.

We sat on a blanket and ate.
Ed cut the cake and we all sang him 'Happy Birthday'.
He said,
'That's a kickass cake, Ange,'
biting into the first slice.

I couldn't keep my eyes off the jungle gym,
wondering when we'd be done
so I could play.
Ed noticed. 'Let's go have fun, Joe!'
He reached for two more slices of cake,
handed one to me,
stuffed the other piece into his mouth.

Then
he grabbed my arm,
        pulled me up.
'God, Angela, you're some baker,' he said.
        And we were off.

    That was a better day.

SIX O'CLOCK

Father Matthew shows up at six.
As Ed is introducing him to Angela and Karen
a yellow phone attached to the wall rings.
The guard answers it,
mumbles into the mouthpiece.
He holds the receiver over his head,
calls over. 'It's Alan Mitchell.'

Angela puts her hand over her mouth.

      Ed shuffles to the phone.

Everyone in the room is silent.

'Yeah. OK.
I understand.
Yeah. OK.
Yup.
OK, thanks, Al.'

Angela goes to Ed, puts a hand on his arm.
'Gotta wait,' Ed says.
'Al's driving up here now. Said he'll explain.'

I exhale;
I've been holding my breath since the phone rang.

Ed looks at the clock over the door.
Six hours left.

Six hours and one minute.

IRREGULAR

Al storms in at seven thirty,
shakes everyone's hands,
takes a seat.

His blue suit is creased.
His tie is undone.

He's out of breath.
He glances at the guard,
       the door.
'I was in the governor's office in Austin earlier
to file the petition for clemency.
As I was doing it,
I looked over at his secretary's desk
and the denial was coming out of the printer.'

Father Matthew sits up. Aunt Karen frowns.

'What does that even mean?' Angela asks.
She twirls her hair
       around and around her
       pointer finger.

Despite the fan it is sweltering in here.
                    I need air
                    but I can't leave.
                    Not now.

'I don't know,' Al says.
'But it's highly irregular and probably illegal.
I asked to speak to the governor personally.
He told me it was a clerical error and that
he'd be getting to our petition
before eleven o'clock.'

'We leave at ten,' Angela says.

Father Matthew mutters beneath his breath,
a prayer,
and Aunt Karen joins him,
a final call
        to God
        to intervene
where man has
                stood aside
                and watched.

TEN O'CLOCK

Before I've time to decide on the last words to say
        to Ed
it's ten o'clock.
A different guard comes in.
She doesn't speak,
stands there seeming sorry for herself,
like she's the one being tortured.

Al stands. 'Time to go,' he says. 'I'll wait outside.'
He grabs an envelope, shoots through the door.
Father Matthew follows along with the guard.

Aunt Karen takes Ed's hand.
'I'm praying for you all the time,' she says.
'And I'm so very, very sorry.'
Ed kisses her forehead and she scurries out,
so
it's just the kids now,
the three of us
alone
for the first time in ten years.

Angela holds the back of a chair.
I steady myself on her arm.

I want to whimper,
feel like collapsing.

But I have to hold it together
        for Ed.

No use him seeing his siblings crumble.

He has to know we're OK.

Ed faces us. 'This isn't the end.
In an hour Heath McDowell
will make a call and you'll be back
tomorrow afternoon
wondering when the hell you get to go home.'
        His voice is wispy;
        he hardly believes it himself.

Ed feels out of reach,
like I'm seeing him from
        across a football field.
Will he hear me if I speak?
Can he understand
        when he's so far away?
'Ed,' I whisper.

'Come here, Joe.' He reaches for me,
takes me in his arms, squeezes.
Then he pulls Angela into us too
and we are silent,
cos nothing can be said now
        that matters
        all that much.

The clock ticks loudly.

I don't know how many minutes pass
but Al returns. 'I'm sorry,' he says.
'They're calling time.'

Ed releases the embrace
        and Angela stumbles,
        saves herself by reaching for my hand.
I hold her up, help her step away from Ed.
She isn't crying.
She sounds like she might be sick.

I reach forward one last time and hold him.
'I'm glad we got this time together,' I say.

Ed pulls away, his eyes swollen with tears.
'Take care of yourselves, OK?'
And then he turns,
puts his back to us completely.

I hold Angela's hand,
      pull her
            out of the room as quickly as I can.

The guard shuts the door.

I fall to the floor.

And from the closed room we can hear Ed.

He is howling
        our names.

WITNESS

Angela collects her bag,
about to follow Father Matthew to the visitors'
cafeteria
in the main prison,
where they'll wait a couple of hours
until the witness gallery is ready.
Angela will watch the state murder Ed,
something she can never unsee,
a movie that will play
for the rest of her life.
'There's no reason to do this,' I tell her.

She is crying,
          snot running into her mouth.
'He can't be alone,' she snivels.

'But *you'll* be alone,' I tell her.

Aunt Karen offers Angela a Kleenex.
'*I'll* be the witness,' she tells us. 'It's the least I can do.'

But Angela is adamant.
She will not relinquish this role.
'He'll be expecting me,' she says.

'Then I'll wait with you,' Aunt Karen insists,
and all three of them
leave through a
heavy metal door.

BELIEF

Nell opens her arms and takes me in.
'Let's go for a drive,' she says.

Behind her,
        protesters' candles blink.
I could join them, as I planned,
but my voice will make no difference.

I'm not in any mood to pray anyway.
I don't believe in God today.

        I don't even believe in people.

IN THE DARKNESS

A hill overlooks the farm.
I drive, Nell grasping my knee.
She pats it now and then, and asks, 'Are you OK?'
I nod, though I'm not.
I'm afraid I might pass out,
                    veer off the road into a ditch,
            vomit all over myself.
I fix my eyes to the road,
focus on the car moving.
If I cause an accident I'll hurt Nell;
            I don't want that.

We stop at the lookout point.
From up here you can see the whole farm –
every rotten thing happening below;
cars and vans come and go,
lights in cells shut out,
            and Section A
            to the right,
            the only part of the prison lit up –
            bright lights against the black.

I reach for the radio. Nell stops me.
'If anything changes, they'll call,' she says,

and she's right; what else will I hear
over the airwaves
but people gunning for Ed?

Nell hands me a beer and a bottle opener,
strokes the back of my neck with her fingertips.
'What can I do?' she asks.

'Nothing,' I say.
        'Just sit in the darkness with me.'

A MINUTE BEFORE MIDNIGHT

Nell and I have had three beers each,
shared a titanic pack of Twizzlers.

My phone pings.
A message from Al:
> Governor denied our appeal
> for a stay. I'm sorry, Joe.
> I'll call you afterwards.
> Al

MIDNIGHT

I stumble out of the car,
breathe in the moist air.

Nell is out the
      passenger side,
        comes to me. 'What was it?'

I hold out my phone; she reads the message.
      'You're going to survive this,' she says.
She tries to wrap her arms around me,
but I step away,
lay my hands flat on the hood,
face the farm, their lights,
and imagine
the strap-down team
      taking Ed from his holding cell
          to the death chamber,
the murmurings of the priest's final prayer,
Angela's face as the curtains open
      and she sees Ed, IVs in his arms,
        head shaved,
            body fastened down
            too tight
            for him to move.

And there's Philip Miller nodding,
giving the go ahead for poisons to be pumped
        into Ed's body.

I stare at the moon,
        round and the colour of oatmeal.
'The moonrise was beautiful all month,' I tell Ed.
'It's beautiful underneath this sky.'

IT IS DONE

Ed is gone.

TIME TRAVEL ME

Time travel me back.
Let me say goodbye again.
A minute more,
      a moment,
a chance to see Ed's face
      alive,
hold his hand like we did when I was a kid –
feel his skin and smell him.

Time travel me back.
Let me relive *any* moment with Ed;
I'll take him at his worst,
      his moodiest.
Anything at all so long as he can hear me.

Time travel me back
so I can say goodbye and mean it.
Give me the final moment again
to use the words no one in our house
ever dared say to one another –
scared of being sappy or overemotional.
Give me the three seconds with Ed
and I will tell him the words and I will mean them.
I will say,
      I love you.

DRIVING HOME

Nell drives and we don't speak.

Every limb is numb
or aching.
My mind is racing
         and then slow.

Never
         again.

                        Never.

Never
         again.

That's when I'll next see my brother.

BODY CURLED UP

I bolt upright on the blow-up mattress
on the living room floor.
'Angela?'
She is standing over me,
body shuddering.
I pull her down
and she lies on her side,
face to the window,
body curled up like a baby.
She starts to shake.
I lie on the sheet next to her,
wrap her in my arms,
do nothing useful at all
except listen to the hurt.

ANOTHER NEXT MONTH

I get up early and
step around the blow-up bed where
Angela is still curled up into a small ball,
asleep,
dressed in her clothes from last night.

The door to the bedroom is closed.
Maybe Aunt Karen is awake,
but if she wanted to talk, she would have come out.

I dress for my run and take off,
down the apartment block stairs,
through the parking lot,
          along Main Street to the edge of town.

Usually this is where I head home,
where the sidewalk ends.
But this morning I keep going
down unlit streets,
past empty fields
and buzzing factories.

I run and run in the pre-dawn light,
not noticing too much the aching in my legs.

And I find the prison,
where I expect to see cameras,
a few remaining protesters holding banners aloft.

But it's finished.
Over.
Like nothing ever happened here.

A janitor collects something from the ground
and throws it into a trash can.
The place is strewn with candy bar wrappers,
cigarette butts,
candle wax.
'The party's over, I guess,' I say to him.

The janitor shrugs.
'They got another party planned for
September sixteenth.'

'Another execution?'

'Sure. Dick Reese got a date last week.'

'I missed that news,' I say.

'Yeah, well,
Dick ain't got a chance in hell.
You know what he did?'

'Does it matter?' I ask.
'Does it really matter what he did?'
and without waiting for an answer,
I turn around and start running.

THE NEWS REPORTS

Philip Miller refuses to make a statement to the media,
but speaking straight into the camera Al says,
'I now have to go and speak with Mr Moon's family.
I wish someone at Governor McDowell's office
would tell me how I explain this to them.
I doubt anyone could.
In any case, all McDowell's team
are probably sound asleep.'

A journalist explains
that Ed's body will remain at the farm
until an autopsy has been carried out.

Only then will he be released to us.

But the autopsy
won't tell the truth –
       which is that my brother was
       murdered.

BELONGINGS

I collect Ed's belongings,
everything tossed untidily into a clear bag.
The guard makes me sign something, then says,
'Plenty of others deserved to go ahead of him,
you know?'
I nod politely
as the warden saunters in.
He gestures for the guard to leave us alone.

'I wanted to say goodbye,' Philip Miller says.
'To give you this –' he hands me a letter –
'and also tell you I'm sorry.
Not officially.
But as a person.
I'm sorry for what's happened here,' he says.

He reaches forward
but he's out of his mind if he thinks
I'm going to let him touch me.
        I step away
        and we watch one another.

When he senses I'm not about to absolve him,
he opens the door for me to leave, and I do,
without another word.

WHAT IS LEFT BEHIND

There's nothing unusual in the bag:
a pair of Adidas high tops;
tatty jeans, the knees faded;
a fake TAG watch;
a wallet with a Walmart card in it;
one dollar and seventy-eight cents in change;
a calendar with happy penguins on it,
check marks counting down his last days
     and circled in red,
       August 18.

I stuff everything back into the bag
and reach into my pocket for the
letter Philip Miller handed me.
It's Ed's handwriting.
His last letter.

THE LAST LETTER

Dear Joe and Ange,

So,

> *you left a half hour ago*
> *and I'm writing cos I*
> *haven't much else to do.*
> *Al is here.*
> *We are waiting to hear from the governor.*
> *Could get the call real soon.*
> *It's five after eleven now.*
> *I got Father Matthew here too.*
> *And he's a good guy even though*
> *he smells like*
> *a bacon and frankincense sandwich.*
> *He keeps reading the Bible*
> *but I can't concentrate on that stuff.*

Thing is,

> *it's real quiet here.*
> *I'm in a new cell next to the chamber.*
> *Just a bench.*
> *No bed or anything.*
> *And they don't allow radios now.*

Thing is,
> I want you to know I'm OK.

I mean,
>> I'm scared.
>> My hand's wobbling a bit writing this
>> but I'm OK.

So,
>> don't worry about me,
>> about how it was
>> if it happens
>> or what I've been through.
>> Think about yourself. Take care of each other.
>> I'm no poet so I don't know how to say the hard stuff
>> but I can still feel the hug you guys gave me
>> before you left.
>> I know I was sticking to you pretty tight
>> but I wanted to remember it
>> and I want you to feel that cling.

You know,
>> I reckon people sit here with a mountain of
>> regrets
>> but I haven't got many.
>> I'm here cos I was tired of being trapped
>> and it didn't work out great but I can't say

I'd change much,
even after everything that's happened.
So,

do all the stuff you want even
if someone tries to deadlock your front door.
Be brave about it.
Open the back door at night
and let in the noises, or hell,
I don't know, run, escape if you have to.
If that's the only way to live.
And if someone tries to stop you,
you tell them you can't save anyone's life
but your own.
OK,

it's almost time.
Guards want to get me ready.
So,

I'm leaving for now.
Thing is,

if I write any more I might quote Oprah and
NO ONE wants that!
Al's back actually.
Hopefully it's good news.
Hope. Ha!

And the thing is,
if it's not good news,
at least I'm free.
We all are.
Love always. Always.
Your brother — Ed xx

THE PAIN

I knew this day was around the corner,
that I should have been prepared
for the coughing,
the heaving in my body,
the tears
that won't stop,

         the scream
         I let out,
the scream that fills up the apartment
and makes Karen come running.
'Joe?'

    I should be ready for this pain,
    but I'm not
    because I never believed
    that Ed would die.

REMEMBERING

Sue arrives with homemade moussaka,
Nell with bottles of wine and water.
No one eats but we drink a lot and talk,
and I tell them about the time Ed dressed up
as a snow queen for Halloween.
He nearly gave Mom a seizure
when she arrived home from work to see a
six-foot-tall guy in drag
      standing in the middle of our kitchen
      frying liver in a pan.

Angela laughs and says, 'Ed loved to dress up.
When you were real small he was Santa.
You remember?
He almost frightened you to death.
And he forgot to bring a present!'

'Of course I remember,' I say,
and for the rest of the night that's what we do:
      we remember the Ed we knew.

RELEASED

They release Ed now they're happy with how he died.
Apparently it was cardiac arrest.
That's what the report says.

TO HOUSTON

Angela and Karen are already on the bus,
pretending not to watch.

'I like the idea of Columbia for college,' Nell says,
lightly punching my arm,
'so I guess I'll see you around New York sometime.
Maybe I'll cheerlead your track and field events …
except I won't.'

'I'll visit when I've got some money,' I say.
I open my backpack, pull out a large bottle of water.
'Want this? I won't be able to take it on the plane.'

She hits me again and it hurts.
'You romantic, Joe Moon.
But you better keep it.
It's a few hours to Houston.
I don't want you dying of thirst.'

The bus wheezes and spits.

Angela raps on the window and waves.
Nell smiles up at her.

'You better go,' she says.

'Sue told me to leave
as soon as this was over.
I have to take her advice.'

Nell waves me away. 'I know you can't stay.
It's just ....'
She bites her lips.

'I know,' I say.
And I do. Of course I do.
'But what about you? You and your dad?'

She shrugs. 'We'll be fine,' she says.

I don't reply.

'We *will*,' she insists.
'Now get out of this shithole before it buries you!'

BACK IN ARLINGTON

The sky is bright blue,
the sidewalks peppered with old bits of gum and
cracked from years of carrying people.

> I go into our house,
> my bedroom,
> the place I used to share with Ed.

My bed is made,
but the blinds are shut,
making it seem like night-time.

Something glitters
on the bookcase.
I follow the glint.

It's a plastic, glow-in-the-dark
crescent moon
no wider than a dime.

I hold it in the palm of my hand.

The arc smiles up at me.

I didn't know I had this in here.
It must have been Ed's from years ago.

I fold my fingers around the plastic piece
and scan the room for other signs of moons or stars,
Ed
hidden in the everyday,
burrowed away in my life forever.

Because,
          hell,
          you never know
          what you might find in the dark.

AUTHOR'S NOTE

I was fifteen years old when I first saw a 1987 BBC documentary called *Fourteen Days in May* about a man called Edward Earl Johnson, whose courage and dignity whilst on death row in Mississippi had a profound and lasting impact on me. *Moonrise* is, in so many ways, inspired by that brave film. It is also inspired by the lawyer representing Johnson at that time, Clive Stafford Smith, now the director of Reprieve and author of *Injustice: Life and Death in the Courtrooms of America*. I urge the reader to see *Fourteen Days in May*, if possible.

I also encourage the reader to seek out *Just Mercy: A Story of Justice and Redemption* by Bryan Stevenson, a book about the American justice system, which hugely influenced this novel. Finally, please do check out the wonderful work done by the Equal Justice Initiative (EJI.org) for death row prisoners, as well as the many other men and women unfairly treated by the system.

ACKNOWLEDGEMENTS

First and foremost, thank you to Maureen Price, my Religious Studies teacher at school, who forced her classes to watch *Fourteen Days in May* despite its devastating effect. She was right about how important it is. She also believed in me way back when, and that faith led to so much.

This novel wasn't easy to complete and would never have seen the light of day had it not been for Brian Conaghan, who read and gave feedback on every version of the project — I owe you so much. Nikki Sheehan, thank you for the inappropriately hilarious encouragement and professional advice.

Thank you to my editors, Zöe Griffiths, Hannah Sandford and Helen Vick, for their patience and hard work, and to my publicist Emma Bradshaw as well as the entire children's team at Bloomsbury — this has been a massive team effort and I love being on your team! Thank you to Julia Churchill, my agent, for it all.

Thanks also to Repforce Ireland, Combined Media, The Big Green Bookshop, CLPE, Children's Books Ireland, CILIP, David O'Callaghan, Hélène Ferey and all my friends and family for being bloody fabulous.

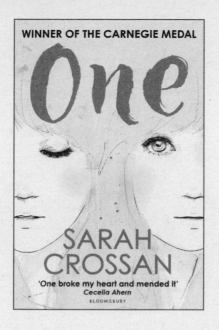

Grace and Tippi don't like being stared and
sneered at, but they're used to it. They're conjoined
twins – united in blood and bone. What they want
is to be looked at in turn, like they truly are two
people. They want real friends. And what about love?
But a heart-wrenching decision lies ahead for Tippi
and Grace. One that could change their lives more
than they ever asked for …

Nicu is so not Jess's type. He's all big eyes and
ill-fitting clothes, eager as a puppy, even when they're
picking up litter in the park for community service.
Appearances matter to Jess. She has a lot to hide.
Nicu shouldn't even be looking at her. His parents are
planning his marriage to a girl he's never met back
home in Romania. But he wants to work hard, do
better, stay here. As they grow closer, their secrets
surface like bruises. And as the world around them
grows more hostile, the only safe place Jess and Nicu
have is with each other.

APPLE
AND RAIN

SHORTLISTED
CILIP
Carnegie
Medal
2015

SARAH CROSSAN

BLOOMSBURY

When Apple's mother returns after eleven years away,
Apple feels whole again. She will have an answer
to her burning question – why did you go?
But just like the stormy Christmas Eve when she left,
her mother's homecoming is bitter sweet.
It's only when Apple meets someone more lost
than she is, that she begins to see things
as they really are.

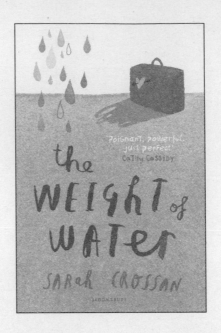

Armed with a suitcase and an old laundry bag,
Kasienka and her mother head for England.
Life is lonely for Kasienka. At home her mother's
heart is breaking; at school friends are scarce.
But when someone special swims into her life,
Kasienka learns that there might be more
than one way for her to stay afloat.